GAME, SET, AND CATCH!

A TAMSIN KERNICK ENGLISH COZY MYSTERY

BOOK 8

LUCY EMBLEM

First Edition 2025

Published by Quilisma Books

ALSO BY LUCY EMBLEM

More mysteries with Quiz, Banjo, and Moonbeam

Where it all began ..

Sit, Stay, Murder!

Ready, Aim, Woof!

Down Dog!

Barks, Bikes, and Bodies!

Ma-ah, Ma-ah, Murder!

Snapped and Framed!

Christmas Carols and Canine Capers! A Howling Good Christmas Mystery!

Game, Set, and Catch!

CHAPTER ONE

"You know what?" Tamsin tossed her dark unruly hair out of her eyes for the fifth time and handed her housemate Emerald a mug of steaming coffee.

"Nope. Not unless you enlighten me," Emerald shifted her large fluffy cream cat Opal a little on her lap, re-arranged the blanket, and smiled as she reached a long languid arm out for her mug. She glanced out of the front windows, "Looks like the Malvern Hills have gone AWOL again - just look at the mist rolling down through the trees!"

Tamsin walked over to the bay window and looked out - at one of her favourite views in all the land. The Malvern Hills rose up beside them, towering over the town. Formed out of the sea seven hundred million years ago, the long granite ridge of hills stood tall and alone in the Severn valley. "Yeah, you can't see the summits at all. It is beautiful though - I love these wintry mists."

"March." Emerald said. "The leaves will be sprinkling the trees with bright green again soon. I'm looking forward to Spring!"

"Me too. Hosing the mud off twelve paws and one pair of wellies every day becomes quite wearing," Tamsin grinned. "Though I usually put them through the stream at the end of a walk - helps a lot. Even better if they get wet before they hit the mud. It doesn't stick then."

"You're full of tricks!" said Emerald, admiringly.

The three dogs had padded into the living room after Tamsin. Quiz, the big dark Border Collie with one lop ear, subsided onto one of the dog beds with a deep satisfied sigh. Banjo, the blue merle Collie, chose to lie on the wooden floor, chin on paws, and kept his blue eyes on his beloved person, while tiny Moonbeam quivered in front of the chair, hopping from one thin leg to another, waiting for the moment she could float up onto Tamsin's lap.

"Hold on, Moonbeam - just going to get another bar of this fire going - it's freezing!" and with a pop and a whoosh, another panel of the gas fire sprang into life. Tamsin sat down in the armchair and patted her lap to encourage Moonbeam to hop up. Then, once the little dog had turned round three times and found a comfortable position, Tamsin - reaching for her coffee and warming her hands round the mug - said, "Well, I've been thinking .."

"Uh-oh."

"No really, I have. I'm not getting any younger, and I know I do loads of walking, and a little of the yoga you've taught me ..."

"Toldya, you should come to class and learn a lot more."

"No thank you. We don't all look like Pre-Raphaelite heroines, like you. Disporting myself in weird postures in flimsy clothing is best done in the confines of my bedroom. Even the dogs cover their eyes with their paws and don't watch."

Emerald smiled. "I know, and you'd rather not do it in front of all those dog training students of yours who are also my yoga students."

"Exactly."

"Sorry, I interrupted you."

Tamsin sat back heavily in the armchair, and sighed loudly. "You see, I think I need to get fitter."

"You're pretty fit already!"

She waved away the comment with her hand. "And possibly do a different activity. With people who don't know who I am, and don't expect me to answer their questions."

"It wouldn't take them long to find out." Emerald removed Opal's kneading claws from her leg and plonked her on the sofa beside her, pulling the blanket back over her lap. "You wouldn't be able to resist dishing out free advice if they spoke disparagingly about their dog."

"You're right," Tamsin sighed. "I can't help it! I'm on a mission to improve dogs' lives, and I can never stay away from it. I can't bear it when people blame their dog, and say they're stupid." She took a swig of coffee and started fondling Moonbeam's huge bat-ears. "It'd be nice to do something different, anyway."

"That's true. So what are you thinking of?"

"We-e-ell," Tamsin leant back in the armchair. 'I was inspired by watching Wimbledon last summer, and I'd love to have a go at tennis."

"Great idea! There's a tennis club in Great Malvern, isn't there?"

"There is. I checked it out. Seems nice enough, but their club night is on a Monday, and that's when I have class at Nether Trotley."

"Can't you book courts at other times?"

"I'm sure you can. But you have to know three other people to play with. It seems that once you're a member you can come to club night. I'd rather just slide in to the club session on my own, you know? Gradually improve - hopefully!"

"Gotcher. Hmm. Perhaps there are other clubs with different days?" Emerald suddenly stopped plaiting her long ash-blonde hair, and thrust one arm up in the air. "I know! I heard Sara chatting to Julia the other night at my yoga class - Sara was back for half-term. They belong to some little club in the sticks in Herefordshire. Julia was saying how much she enjoyed it, specially as she thought she was useless at tennis and nobody was nasty to her about it."

"Oh, that sounds just the thing! I'll be useless too. Batted a few balls around in the garden with my mother, and at school from time to time. But otherwise - useless!"

"Ask Sara about their place."

Tamsin had her head bent over her phone. "Already on it ... there!

I've sent her a text. I'm looking forward to this already! In fact, I'm going to dig out the kit!" And so saying, she tipped Moonbeam off her lap and strode out to the back garden, followed by three excited dogs, to check the shed.

Emerald shook her head fondly and scooped up Opal for another cuddle. It was a fair while before a cobweb-haired Tamsin came back in to the living room with a gust of cold air and a wooden racquet in a tennis press held in her grubby hands.

"What did you find?"

Tamsin held the dusty racquet up in the air. "This," she said glumly, "and these." She held out her hand with two greyish-white tennis balls which had clearly fed an army of moths.

"I'd say the balls are for the bin. And the racquet .." Emerald looked at the racquet in its press, one of the strings snapped, its leather handle faded and fraying, "You could probably get money for this ... from a museum," she grinned.

Tamsin smiled back and sat down again. "It was my Mum's. She used to belong to a tennis club. Somehow I never got involved." She leant the racquet against the wall and said, "Wonder what sort I should get?"

"Perhaps you should wait till you've found somewhere to play, then you can ask one of the people there. They should know."

"You're right. I have to wait. Get things in order." She drummed her fingers on the arm of her chair, itching to get started.

"I love that you're so impetuous! When you get one of your grand ideas, you have to have it *now!*"

"There are upsides to that, you know," Tamsin said defensively. "Think how I got my dog training school started in the first place. It was by doing. Then I found out just how much I had to learn and set about learning it. I think I might still be studying if I'd done it the other way round."

"Bit like me, really. I'd been doing yoga since I was six years old. I just had to learn how to deal with people effectively and make it a business. And you've helped me a lot there, Tamsin." Opal, having gone to inspect the strange object Tamsin had brought in, gave a tiny sneeze, her head freezing in mid-air, then clambered back onto Emerald's lap, her body temperature having dropped a critical one-tenth of a degree. Emerald smoothed out the blanket for her.

"I'm just a few years ahead of you, that's all. But I've sure learnt some tricks of the trade!" She took a gulp of her coffee. "Erk! Stone cold! I'll make another." But before she could get up, her phone woofed at her with Moonbeam's bark. "That's Sara's ringtone, hmm, let's see ... Yes! They have club night on Wednesdays." She looked up brightly, "I can do Wednesdays!"

She read on, "Umm, ah, and they're keen to get new members too," she smiled broadly, as everything began to fall into place. "Wonder where it is?" She tapped out a message to Sara, and after a moment read her reply. "It's called Tom's." She frowned, "Funny name for a club. It's over towards Stretton Grandison."

"Heading out towards Welsh Wales. Will you need a passport?"

"Very droll. It's this side of Hereford. Ah, Sara says to just turn up on Wednesday night. *They're ever so nice,* she says. Um, Julia should be there, but Sara's still at college till Easter, more or less. Apparently the club will advise on a racquet. Er .. she reckons they can lend me one for the evening." She tapped a quick reply and cast the phone aside. "Better look out some tennis shoes too. Think my trainers will do?"

"You can ask them that too. But they'll do for Wednesday, I'm sure. This is exciting!"

"A new enterprise. A clean sheet. Friendly people. Carefree tennis. Can't wait!"

But, being Tamsin, she should have foreseen how differently things were to turn out.

CHAPTER TWO

"I think that's a splendid idea, my dear," Charity returned her teacup to its saucer and dabbed her lips with the paper serviette with 'The Cake Stop' emblazoned on it. Tamsin, Emerald, Feargal, and Charity were having their usual break after loading their bags with local food from the weekly Farmers' Market. It was the most picturesque affair, the stands with their gaily-striped green and white covers, perched on a little street below the towering Hills. Sometimes it was held in the grounds of Malvern Priory, amidst the majestic trees - always with the backdrop of the Malvern Hills, protective, permanent, behind them..

"I remember they used to have tennis parties up at the big house in Middle Trotley," Charity went on. "Of course, I wasn't invited. It was for the children and young people from wealthy families. But I can remember peeping through the hedge to watch with some of my friends from the village. Occasionally a ball would come flying out into the road, and it was 'finders keepers'."

"Charity, I'm appalled at this blatant thievery!" laughed Tamsin.

"You never saw young Joe Bucket run so fast as when he grabbed a ball and hightailed it home! The other boys and some of us girls would chase him - but he always got away."

"Hard to imagine Joe as a boy," said Emerald, thinking of the elderly gardener and horseman they knew now, with his stooping gait and gnarled hardworked hands.

"He was a wiry little fellow .." Charity said dreamily.

"Tales of the Trotleys," pronounced Feargal, who'd been working his way through two toasted sandwiches and was now starting on his chocolate cake, a delicious squishy concoction oozing dark buttercream and adorned with a forest of chocolate curls, for all the world looking like a pile of logs. Really the bakers Dodds & Co - aka the Three Furies - had excelled themselves. Tamsin hoped he'd finish it soon so she could stop ogling it. "One of these days you should write it all down, Charity. In fact, why not write something for the *Malvern Mercury* like Tamsin does? I can talk to my Features Editor - and he could dig out some lovely old photos from the newspaper's library."

"Oh no, dear, I really don't think so. I'd have to tell the truth, and a lot of the people are still living ..." The three friends all burst out laughing.

"And you don't want to get sued for libel!" Tamsin chirruped as she dipped her finger in the froth of her coffee and offered it to Moonbeam, who was lying down with Charity's fluffy brown dog Muffin, her special friend. Their mat was carefully positioned between Tamsin's and Charity's chairs, with a great view of all the comings and goings on the street outside. It was lunchtime, and Great Malvern was busy, with office and shop workers taking their lunch break, and shoppers enjoying a leisurely chat before scurrying up the hill to the Farmers' Market to fill their shopping bags with what had not been plundered by Tamsin and her friends.

Moonbeam licked the creamy froth from her lips and suddenly cocked her huge ears to the pavement outside the window. She stood, her mouth partly open and her tail swishing merrily. Tamsin followed her gaze, then waved vigorously as she saw who it was.

"Look, it's Sara! The very person .." and she got up and shuffled her chair round a little more towards Charity, to make room for the smiling newcomer.

"Hello Stranger!" said the chirpy Sara to Feargal as she peeled off her woolly gloves and unwound the bright stripey scarf from her neck. "Haven't seen you for ages."

"And what brings you here today? Not at college?" responded Feargal as he jumped up to fetch a chair for her.

"Home for the weekend, so I'm picking up a few hours at *Flying Pedals*. There's a whole load of new season's bikes that need to be entered on the shop's system, apparently. So I thought I'd drop over to see you all!" She nodded towards Charity and Tamsin's laden bags of vegetables and bread against the wall. "I reckoned you'd be here for the Market. I'll just go and get myself a coffee. Any refills needed?"

"No thanks," said Tamsin, holding up her still half-full mug. She'd never let a student pay for her coffee. The others followed her lead and shook their heads.

When Sara returned with her mug of coffee, Feargal asked her, "Will you be shopping at the Market too?"

"No need! We have the Bishop's Green cottagers keeping us well-supplied with home-grown grub. And of course we have some from the estate gardens, as well as pheasant and venison from our shoots."

Tamsin winced at the mention of shooting birds - it was so unfair! The beautiful creatures didn't stand a chance against a gun. How anyone could consider it a sport baffled her. And she knew Sara felt the same, so had no need to say anything.

"So you're skiving off school to earn money at the bike shop," grinned Feargal. "What about your hoss?"

"Crystal's great. A friend of mine is looking after her at College for the weekend. We run a little rota, minding each others' horses so we can get a break. Showjumping entry fees add up, you know! I need the cash."

"Actually, you're the very person I wanted to see," Tamsin turned earnestly to her. "About this tennis club .."

"Oh, it's great fun! I'm glad you'll be coming too, Tamsin. Only I won't be there on club night till the Easter break."

"So what club is this?" asked Feargal, his reporter's nose twitching.

"It's called Tom's. No idea why. It's not so far from Bishop's Green - over towards Stretton Grandison."

Charity shifted in her chair, and Tamsin looked expectantly at her. "Go on, Charity, spill the beans!"

"I do happen to know a little about Tom's," she began diffidently.

"Of course you do!" laughed Emerald.

"Now dear, don't tease." Charity tried to look offended, but failed. Rather her cheeks dimpled and her eyes sparkled.

"Tell us!" chorused Tamsin and Sara.

Charity took a sip of tea and began. "Everyone knew of Thomas Wainwright. He was Hereford's tennis champion. He played at Wimbledon a number of times - quite the star - and even went abroad to compete. That was unusual, in those days. He lived in a tiny hamlet between Castle Frome and Stretton Grandison. And in the grounds of his large house he built three tennis courts. One was grass and one was a hard court. I can't remember what the third was .."

"Clay? The red stuff?" prompted Sara.

"Yes, that was it. He needed to practice on all the different sorts of courts the competitions were held on."

"Makes sense," nodded Tamsin, thinking of the different surfaces encountered in various dog competitions, and how you had to get your dog used to them.

"Now this was back in the day - his heyday was in the thirties. And of course there were no tournaments during the war. I gather tennis players earn huge sums these days - it certainly wasn't the case back then! They were *amateurs,* so they didn't win any money at all. Once he retired, the courts were in danger of falling into disuse, so he invited the villagers to help themselves, and in return they looked after the upkeep."

"What a good idea!" exclaimed Emerald.

"And in his will he left the three tennis courts and the little wooden pavilion he'd built there, to the village, in perpetuity. There was one condition: it had to be open to all - he was very firm on that. He didn't want people excluded from the possibility of playing his favourite game."

"As *you* were, from the tennis parties in Middle Trotley," said Feargal.

"Indeed. But even the cost of a tennis racquet was quite high in those days, for the likes of us. So I never went to the club myself. And it would have been quite a hike on the bicycle. But that's why it's affectionately known as Tom's. In gratitude."

"What a lovely story," Tamsin sighed.

"Now, at last, I know why it's called Tom's!" said Sara. "I did wonder why a tennis club was built out in the middle of nowhere. But I do believe there's a fund for tennis gear for those who can't manage it, now you mention it. "

"There you go. Charity knows everything - you should have known that!" grinned Tamsin. "So does it cost much to join?" she asked.

"Hardly anything. I always thought it very reasonable and thought maybe it was because it's so rural. But now I see that it was laid down in the gift. What a great man!" She took a mouthful of coffee, then went on, "Of course, Dad pays for a family membership for us, so it doesn't cost me a bean. But I know our neighbour Julia appreciates that it's an accessible fee, being on her own. She takes Oliver and Francine sometimes, when she can tear them away from their screens."

"Well I'm really looking forward to next Wednesday."

"All set with your whites?" Feargal grinned.

"I haven't even got a racquet yet! I don't know what sort to buy."

"Don't worry," said Sara quickly, "Someone will lend you one - and you'll get plenty of advice on what to get and where to get it."

The sight of Feargal's chocolate cake had been nagging her all this while and at last it got to Tamsin. "I'm going to celebrate my forthcoming fitness!" she said, "Who'd like some cake?"

And they all declined, laughing, so she pigged a slice of the mouthwatering creation all by herself.

CHAPTER THREE

The day of Tamsin's tennis debut at Tom's had come round. But she didn't have much time to think about it - the evenings were still getting dark early and she had three home visits to fit in first, after some training with her own dogs.

"Wonder how they play tennis in the dark?" she suddenly said to the dogs, who looked up expectantly, hoping this question might relate to games or food. "Course! Silly me. They must have floodlights." Tamsin gave a short laugh and carried on packing her training bag, loading it up with various leads, harnesses, and toys, and a pot full of tiny cubes of cheese and sausage. "How lovely to have a floodlit space - think of all the dog training I could do with you lot! That's the one thing that's missing from this little house - a twenty acre field!" She paused for a moment as her eyes gazed into space, and she added, "I could have my own dog training school premises ... I could expand the school, hold more classes - perhaps teach Tracking, or Agility ..." Then with a shake of her shoulders, she said, "but that's never going to happen." The dogs waved their tails encouragingly at her ramblings, and carried on watching the packing for a while. Then with a sigh they went back to their dozing. They'd already had a tramp across the Common - getting drenched in the process - and two of them had training sessions lined up for today too.

Banjo's lesson was going to be devoted to searching. For his Search & Rescue work, up on the Malvern Hills, he had mostly to find lost people. And he was even learning how to find dead people. But sometimes finding *objects* was helpful in locating the missing person. Fortunately his cadaver searching hadn't come into play yet - nobody had got that lost on the nearly ten mile stretch of the Hills. So, as it was still raining heavily, it was a game of hide and seek in the house. Tamsin had a sealed bag containing items that other people had handled for her, and she used tongs to hide them so that they didn't get her scent on too. Essentially Banjo was searching for something that was out of place, that didn't belong. He wasn't searching for anything specific.

And didn't he love it! It was a challenge to Tamsin to find new places to hide the items, and she actually put some at table height for the first time. It was comical to see Banjo lifting his nose from the floor, extravagantly and noisily air-scenting near the table bearing the pen she'd put there.

Banjo did really well, and even located the glove she'd placed the other side of a closed door. His noisy sniffing and snorting at the gap under the door was quickly followed by his single bark - his marker for when he found something out on the Hills.

Feeling pleased with her dog's progress, Tamsin set off to her home visits. She had quite a collection of dogs and owners today. As so often, it was the owners' misinterpretation of what their dogs were doing that had resulted in what they thought was a problem. Like the huge Great Dane bought by a trendy couple who'd seen one in a film, who thought the sofa was his as he'd been encouraged to sleep there when a young puppy, and now resented with a growl being asked to get off. The owners thought he'd gone vicious, but he was only requesting to be left on the sofa in peace. It hadn't been hard to encourage the dog to make a better decision and choose his own comfy bed.

Or the terrier she visited next, who was on the go all day, never catching up on sleep, and was ragged and unco-operative by suppertime.

This was a question of teaching the owner some management and timetabling skills.

And her final visit was to a puppy whose owner's legs were so covered in bites and scratches that she'd taken to wearing wellington boots all day long, inside the house. The pup simply needed to learn a better way to play.

It never ceased to amaze her what messes people got themselves into, and what they were then prepared to put up with. Until one day it got too bad, and she would be called in. And she always looked at the dog's behaviour from the dog's point of view. Dogs weren't 'stubborn' or 'doing it on purpose'! They simply did the best they could with the - often non-existent - training they'd been given.

"Ah well," Tamsin said much later to Quiz - who had accompanied her in the car so that after her last session she could work the track she'd laid two hours before, between the other two visits - "it's good that they came to me and not someone who'd just slap an electric shock collar on the poor dog." She shuddered at the thought of the torture dogs suffered at the hands of those looking for a quick fix, who preferred to punish rather than teach. "Here we are! Let's get some fresh air and work this track. Good thing there's been a break in the rain for the last couple of hours, or it would be quite difficult." As ever Quiz appeared to understand every word, her eyes bright with anticipation as she saw her tracking bag being thrown onto Tamsin's shoulder.

And they went through the gate to the private field she was allowed to use when the horses were not occupying it, and set to. Like most places around the Malverns, the field was on the side of a hill, so it was hard going. Quiz followed the track intently and recovered all the small articles Tamsin had placed as she walked - a twist of twine, a plastic lid, a spark plug. This was another form of searching, but different from what she'd been doing with Banjo earlier.

"You dogs and your noses!" she smiled happily as she removed Quiz's tracking harness and wound up her thirty-foot rope line. "You are just so much cleverer than we are." Quiz accepted the ruffle on her head with a smile. "Good thing we teamed up together, eh? Dogs and humans, I mean. Of course it's wonderful that you and I teamed up personally!" And they trotted together back to the car, in complete harmony, Quiz still panting from her exertions and enjoyment.

So she turned the *Top Dogs* van homeward, to a welcoming warm house, with welcoming warm dogs, warm cat, and oh-so-cool housemate.

"Aren't you off on your new venture this evening?" asked Emerald, unwinding her long legs that she had tucked up under her on the couch.

"I am! But I'm going to eat something first. Don't want to go flaking out with starvation as I leap for a dramatic smash," Tamsin smirked. Then she frowned, "Not really sure what to wear .."

"Something stretchy. Got any stretchy trousers? Tracky bottoms? What about those black ones you wore when you came to my yoga class that time?"

"Oh yes! I'll dig something out. It's pretty chilly, but the rain seems to have eased up for the day." And after a snack, and a kiss for each dog's nose, she set off nervously for her first tennis session.

CHAPTER FOUR

Tamsin could see the floodlit courts as she drove down the narrow Herefordshire back roads from Fromes Hill. The weather had at last relented and settled on a damp murkiness, but without any active rain. Then, losing sight of them in the black night, the road ahead lighted only by her headlights, she completely missed the wooded hill above her to the left, and the 15th Century fortified manor house up an imposing drive to her right. But, following the directions from her satnav, she arrived. Once she'd located the exact place - never easy to find a remote new place in the countryside in the dark, but helped by those floodlights! - she pulled into the car park area along the front of the hedge, pleased to see there were several cars there already.

And stepping through the metal gate, which swung shut with a clang behind her, the first person she saw was Julia, who welcomed her enthusiastically, young Oliver bouncing towards her brandishing his racquet.

"Tamsin! Are you going to play tennis with us?" he said, standing next to his mother, almost the same height as her now.

"Tamsin's coming to try us out," soothed Julia.

"Where's your racquet?" demanded Oliver. But before Tamsin could open her mouth, Julia despatched Oliver to find his friend Paddy.

"Come with me," she said. "Sara told me you'd be coming and you'd need some gear. Let's go and find Gavin." She led the way along the path past the three as-yet-empty courts and towards a comical caricature of a tennis pavilion.

It was small and painted dark green, with ornamental fascia boards - rather like a traditional English railway station. It appeared to be made of clapboard, with a covered verandah in front for watching the tennis, and a double door into the main room.

"The toilets are down there," Julia pointed to a separate, more recent, wooden building a little way further up down the path.

Passing a grim-faced woman in tennis gear, Julia chirruped, "Evening Lesley!" and hurried on. Tamsin paused and smiled awkwardly at the woman, who glowered back at her. Coming back and grabbing her elbow, Julia propelled Tamsin into the pavilion. "Gavin! This is Tamsin."

Gavin smiled broadly, his teeth shining white in his suntanned face. And surely that hair was dyed black? "Ah, Tamsin. I'm told I have to look after you." He spoke pleasantly, aiming to put her at her ease. "You're looking for a tennis racquet, am I right?"

"Yes please - just for today. If you tell me what to get I can buy one during the week. But I thought I'd better find out from an expert," she smiled back at him, trying to rein in her distaste. He really did look a bit creepy!

"No trouble. Let me see - show me your hand." Tamsin spread her right hand out in front of him, somewhat puzzled. Gavin held her fingers and turned her hand over.

"I'd guess that's a three grip. They can measure you properly in the shop - but we don't have many spare racquets here." He jumbled some racquets around in a big bucket. "Here you go! This one'll do you for now."

Tamsin took the racquet and held the handle in the middle.

"Like this," said Gavin, grabbing another racquet and placing his hand in the correct position, towards the end. Tamsin did as bidden, and frowned. Oh, this felt odd!

"Don't worry, you'll get used to the feel of it. I suggest you get started knocking up with Julia and a couple of the others over there on the hard court. Let's see what you do naturally. We can always arrange coaching for you later, if you like."

And so saying, he turned to fill in a note in the club book. Julia led Tamsin, swinging her new racquet to get the feel of it, to the court. "Gavin's the head coach," she told her. "He's ever so nice."

"Who was that we passed on the way?" asked Tamsin, still wondering about the sour-faced woman.

Julia lowered her voice. "Oh, that's Lesley. She's the Club Treasurer, for our sins. Always looks as though she's been sucking a lemon. Don't mind her." They entered the court, where two players had started knocking up already. "Hi, Margaret! Hello, Victoria! This is Tamsin - she's joining us for the evening."

Here Tamsin got a great welcome, especially from Victoria. Sharing the same side of the net as Julia she anxiously awaited a ball to come her way. And when it did, she gave a mighty heave ... and missed it entirely.

"Don't worry, Tamsin," Margaret called from the other side of the net. "We all started once. Just keep going - remember to watch the ball right onto your racquet!"

After a little while Tamsin was striking the ball more often than she was missing it. Though she did feel as if she had lead boots on! And with heaps of encouragement from the other three players she found herself thoroughly enjoying herself. After twenty minutes' play, with some arcane scoring system going on which she struggled to keep up with - all those fifteen-love's and deuces, not to mention lets and sudden deaths - they headed back to the pavilion. She found herself well warmed up, and peeled off one of her outer layers.

"That was fun!" she puffed, as they stepped up onto the verandah.

"I can see you enjoyed it! At this time of year we can't use the grass court," explained Julia, "so we have to be sure to give everyone a go on the two courts we can use. Our court's free now, Toto." And with a cheery nod from the Toto Julia had addressed, two men and two different ladies got up to take their place on the hard court.

Tamsin studied the noticeboard. It clearly hadn't been updated for a while, bearing notices about the winners of the league competitions the previous summer. Along with some instructions about remembering to lower the nets after playing, and the phone numbers of the committee members, there was a poster for a lost cat. It had been there so long that three of its four drawing pins had been pinched and it dangled from just one. Its edges were curling round and the colours very faded, so that the cat appeared lilac with yellow eyes. Tamsin hoped the cat had long since returned home, gave herself a quick mental shake and turned to Julia.

"Where's Oliver?"

"He and Paddy are over there on the clay. There's a couple of other youngsters with him."

"So who were those people just going out to play?"

"Ah, sorry - they rushed off before I could introduce you. You can meet them all later. There'll be time to chat at the end of the evening too. We're very sociable here!" she smiled happily.

Tamsin was glad to see Julia looking so settled and content. A different story from how she was when she first called Tamsin in to help with her reactive Schnauzer Romeo. Tamsin thought back to all the carryings-on with the bows and arrows in Julia's little village, smiled gently at the memory, and - pulling herself back to the present - she asked after Romeo.

Detailing his latest escapades, and how much better he was now, kept Julia going until Oliver and Paddy came up to the verandah. Paddy lurked at the foot of the steps as Oliver went up to his mother.

"We've had enough, Mum," he said as he slumped into a chair. "Paddy hit three balls into the trees."

"You'd better go and find them then," retorted Gavin, emerging through the double doors to join them. "Fetch a carrier bag and off you go."

And, dragging himself to his feet, off went Oliver. They could see him picking up Paddy and the other two children on the way to the row of fir trees and hedging.

"That should keep them amused for quite a while," Julia grinned. "They usually come back with quite a haul."

"Will they be able to see in the trees?"

"They'll manage. They always do. And the adults never want to go hunting for balls, so they're quite useful really. Any really good balls go back in the pavilion. The rest they can have."

Tamsin thought of Charity, and Joe Bucket, chasing after tennis balls flung out from the tennis parties all those years ago. Clearly tennis balls were valuable currency still for children. "Does Romeo like tennis balls?"

"Not as much as his frisbee! But he likes to bounce one down the stairs, run to the bottom to catch it, then take it up to the top of the staircase again to nudge it down with his nose. It's fun to watch!"

"Love that! Your Romeo is quite a character!" Feeling the temperature dropping now she was cooling down, Tamsin put her jumper back on, and found that she too was feeling content.

"This is a very pleasant way to spend an evening," she said. "Will we get to play again?"

Victoria was getting up from her seat. "Certainly! Fancy a go on the clay, Tamsin?" she said.

"Sure! What's the difference from the hard court we were just on?"

"It tends to play a bit slower, and the ball bounces higher."

"Unlike the grass where the ball has a really low bounce," put in Gavin.

"And sometimes hardly bounces at all!" added Margaret with a rueful expression. "Come on, let's try you out there."

"I had no idea the surface is so important .." said Tamsin, realising there was a lot more to this game than she'd realised.

And as they set off to continue this voyage of discovery, Tamsin literally bumped into Lesley again, this time just coming round the corner.

"Oops, sorry!" she said, jumping aside.

Lesley stared at her for a moment, then carried on walking to the pavilion. "Gavin!" she called out. "A word, please."

Tamsin watched her walking away.

"C'mon," said Julia. "Don't mind Lesley. She's probably a bit bats in the belfry."

"But harmless," said Margaret. "Don't you worry about her at all."

CHAPTER FIVE

It was quite a while later when the foursome wound up their game on the clay court, and fetched up back at the pavilion. Tamsin was glad it was over - she could already feel unaccustomed muscle aches from this new activity. She rubbed her right shoulder gingerly.

"You'll feel a bit stiff tomorrow morning," the friendly Gavin cruised up beside her. His breath smelled sweet. "But it'll ease off fast enough. How did you enjoy your first session?"

"Loved it!" said Tamsin. "But I think the other three were very patient. I hope I didn't spoil their game."

"We all have to start somewhere, and you picked three nice friends to play with there." He looked speculatively over to the other four, returning from the hard court, another four already taking their place and starting to play. "Some people are far more competitive." He frowned as the two women from the foursome walked past him, deep in conversation, discussing the last point they'd lost, dissecting the play, the thin older one clearly apportioning blame. The younger, plumper, one looked crestfallen and said nothing more.

"Who's for tea?" boomed Margaret. "Come and help yourself. There's a fresh pot, milk, sugar, spoons ..."

"Coffee for me, please, Margaret. Don't worry, I'll do it!" Victoria set about making herself one, and after raising an enquiring eyebrow at Tamsin, picked up another mug and made two. They settled themselves at the back of the verandah as the other four berated each other in quasi-jocular fashion over their game.

"You don't miss much, do you, Glenda?" said Bryan, tall and bearded with thick glasses, as he stowed his racquet in his very large, colourful, tennis bag - big enough for at least four racquets.

"Glenda plays in the League!" Toto called across admiringly to the newcomer. Tamsin smiled back, attempting to look impressed.

"Amanda and I are going to enter the ladies doubles next week, aren't we, Amanda." Glenda's baggy shorts flapped round her thin legs as she strutted about the pavilion.

Amanda nodded dutifully, her chubby cheeks dimpling as she drank from her water bottle. She appeared to have been poured into *her* shorts. Tamsin wondered how someone with such a large bottom could be any good at tennis at all. Then she thought about the huge chocolate cake she'd wolfed at The Cake Stop at the weekend and blushed at her judging.

"You'll probably win!" Toto fawned.

"You in the men's doubles?" asked Glenda, accepting the compliment as her due.

"Yes. Bryan and I are going to give it a shot."

"You'll need to pay attention to your volleys," she began. "You were very slow to some of them. Your court position was all wrong ..."

Tamsin turned to Victoria and spoke quietly as Glenda's lecture continued, "They sound awfully good."

"Oh," replied Victoria, equally quietly. "Glenda thinks she's the bees' knees. She *is* quite good," she conceded, grudgingly. "But she'll always find a reason not to be put in a four with the likes of me. Cut above, you know?"

"Definitely not with the likes of me, then!" laughed Tamsin, thinking, 'There's always one. Always someone who's self-important. But the rest of them are nice.'

"Here, help yourself," said Margaret, waving a plastic container with lots of cut-up pieces of tray-baked chocolate cake. Tamsin made the mistake of accepting a slab, and regretted it as she bit into the dry cake. If you're going to pile in calories, at least they should be moist, succulent, wickedly-good calories, she thought, and pictured for a moment one of the Three Furies' wonderful soft creamy cakes at The Cake Stop.

"Margaret looks after us," said Victoria, unfastening the scrunchy from her hair and slipping it on her wrist, allowing her blonde curls to fall loose on her shoulders. "Bit of a mother hen really," she chuckled.

"Now Tamsin," said Gavin, coming over to join them. "How did you get on with that racquet?"

"Oh, I think it was fine - I'm not really sure .." She held the racquet out for him to take back.

"You seemed to be making a good start. I was watching you!" He gave a leery grin, and Tamsin felt herself pulling away. "Here's what you should look for." Tucking the racquet under his arm, he handed her a piece of paper. "I wrote down some details for you, and some suggested brands. They're all sorts of prices. I suggest you try the sports shop in Hereford - or there's one in Malvern too." He took back the paper and scribbled some more words onto it. "A decent bit of kit will make playing a lot more pleasurable, you know," his shiny white teeth all came on show again.

"Thank you! Will I say you sent me?"

"You can try, but I don't think it'll make much difference," he guffawed, looking around at the others for answering laughter. But the most he got was a slight smirk from Victoria.

"Here's your tea, Glenda," Margaret said, handing a mug to Glenda.

"Did you put sugar in?" Glenda sniffed the mug suspiciously and glowered at Margaret.

"Oh sorry," Margaret replied ingenuously, "Have you given up sugar?"

"How do you think I stay this fit?" demanded Glenda, handing back the mug. "I'll fetch my own, thanks."

"Golly!" whispered Tamsin to Victoria. "I thought this club was meant to be friendly."

"It is really. There are lots more people who come as the weather improves." She turned to face Tamsin. "I'm afraid we're stuck with Glenda, but as long as Lesley's the Treasurer she won't be getting a place on the committee, I'm glad to say, despite the fact that Toto keeps nominating her."

"So we have a use for our grumpy Treasurer," Tamsin grinned. "Oh! I guess she'll be wanting to talk to me, to sign up?"

"That can wait till next week, when you've got your new racquet. In fact Neil will be back by then, and he usually deals with memberships. He's the Club Secretary. You'll like him - everyone loves Neil."

"Oh good! Where is he now?"

"Skiing. He's super-fit. He plays doubles a lot with Jonathan. Sure you'll like him too - lovely guy."

"Jonathan?" The wheels in Tamsin's head were turning.

"Jonathan the Cider guy! Have you not come across him yet? He brings flagons to the summer barbecue."

"Ah yes, I do know who you mean. Yes - nice guy." She nodded, thinking warmly of Jonathan, whom she'd helped with his shy Springer Spaniel Teal around the time of the Farmers' Market contamination dramas. "And I can imagine him being good at tennis, too."

"He is! Don't worry, things will hot up - as the weather does. Tonight's not representative - except for us four!"

"Yes, I really enjoyed playing with you. Oh, look - here are the boys coming back."

"Their bag is bulging!"

"And they've got leaves and twigs stuck in their hair," Tamsin laughed, as Oliver and Paddy trudged up the verandah steps, carrying the large carrier bag between them. Two smaller boys followed them.

"That's a splendid haul, darling," said Julia, reaching for the bag. "Fun getting them?"

"Should have brought Romeo! He'd love to hunt for all these," he said as he held out the bag of tennis balls, some of which looked as though they were fit for the bin after lying in the damp hedgerow for months.

Julia peered at the haul. "So let's have a look at what you found". She started to rummage in the bag. "I think that one and that one could be donated to Romeo's toy-basket," she said, pointing to two of the dirtiest and barest balls.

Oliver puffed up his chest with pride. "It was cool, Mum. The ones wedged high up in the trees I couldn't reach, but Alfie and Mo are much smaller so they could get up through the branches."

"Well done Mohammed, well done Alfie!" Julia leaned over to look past the two bigger boys at the younger, wirier pair. They were quiet lads but grinned back at her, Alfie hopping from one foot to the other, quite unable to keep still, as tiny leaves dropped from his clothes.

"We definitely won't want this one back!" Julia pulled out a some- what bald ball with green stains and tossed it to Oliver.

"Can I have one too?" pleaded Paddy.

"Here, let's give the bag to Gavin. He can pick out anything worth keeping for the club and you can all share what's left. Fair?"

"Fair," chorused Oliver and Paddy, while the two smaller boys started to bounce with excitement.

The bag was passed to Gavin, who set about examining it straight away. "You guys are terrific!" he said, "Go get yourself a drink and some- thing to eat. I'll be back in a moment."

The boys bustled up to the table where Margaret, who clearly knew them well, was in her element catering for them, and they were very happy to hoover up the rest of the dry cake.

Tamsin could contain herself no longer, and once the boys were out of earshot she asked Julia, "Do the children play with Romeo with tennis balls?"

"They do, yes. They've been pestering me to buy one of those ball- throwers, but I think everyone's greenhouses would get smashed, so I've said no."

"That's just as well. Look, you wouldn't believe the number of injuries I come across from people using those things - shoulders, neck, wrists ..."

"From using the stick?" Julia waved her arm as if hurling a ball, waggled her wrist back and forth, and looked puzzled.

"Oh no, I mean the *dog's* shoulders, neck and wrists!" laughed Tamsin. "They go far too fast, land badly, turn dangerously .. you're safer just tossing the ball to Romeo to catch. Tennis balls do have the advantage of being hollow - those solid rubber balls they sell in pet shops are deadly too: they get stuck in the dog's throat."

"I had no idea dogs' toys could be so dangerous!" Julia nodded thoughtfully.

"You seem to know a lot about this," the cold voice of Glenda cut in. "Are you a vet?"

Tamsin cursed herself. She'd meant to keep her work out of this new hobby, but it was too much a part of her to separate. She took a deep breath and turned to Glenda.

"No, I'm a dog trainer," she smiled.

"Oh. Not qualified to give veterinary advice then."

At that moment Tamsin was rescued by Toto calling, "Glenda sweetie!" and Glenda marched off to join him at the other end of the pavilion.

"Don't mind her," urged Julia quietly, "she doesn't have a dog anyway."

"I wouldn't give her a dog *flea* to look after, never mind a dog," whispered Victoria. Then more loudly she said, "That's really interesting Tamsin - thank you! I've learned something today. I'll tell my brother. He has a dog."

Gavin came back to Julia - and it seemed to Tamsin that he was leaning unnecessarily closely over her - with the bag with just a few balls left in. He'd been careful to make sure the number was divisible by four, and the boys scurried over to divide their spoils. Julia watched to ensure the smaller boys got their fair share as they stuffed the pockets of their shorts. It was time for everyone to call it a night and head home.

CHAPTER SIX

Sure enough, when Tamsin got out of bed the next morning she was aching in lots of new places.

"Oof," she said to the dogs as she lowered her legs to the floor. The younger two scurried around, eager to start the new day, while the more sensitive Quiz rested her chin on Tamsin's knees, her brown eyes gazing soulfully up at her. "It's ok, Quizzy. Give me a moment to find out which limbs are working, and we'll go downstairs." She blinked as she leant forward to draw back a corner of the curtain. "Ouch! It's bright out there."

Letting the curtain drop, she stretched her arms out, stood up and stretched each leg, carefully cataloguing where she was stiff. And sending the dogs safely down the stairs before her, as always, she plodded down slowly behind them.

"What's up with you?" asked Emerald, as she went to let the dogs out to the garden.

"Too many brilliant shots, too much running about." Tamsin went over to inspect the kettle. "I was trying to serve like Rafael Nadal. I had no idea quite how difficult it is," she grinned.

"Chump!" snorted Emerald with amusement. "Here, I'll do the coffee while you get this lot fed. Then I'll do some stretching with you."

"Thanks. I'll be fine once I've had some breakfast. Got a few home visits today. That'll keep me busy!"

It was a bright March morning with no wind. "Let's have our coffee in the garden," said Emerald. "We'll soon warm up with the exercises I'll give you!"

The dogs were very happy with this arrangement, and snoofled about in the bushes while Emerald led Tamsin in some stretchy recovery, to the tune of Tamsin's groans and ouches, and even an "Ow-wow!". As Emerald wafted and floated so gracefully, Tamsin became more and more aware of her clumsy plodding and wobbling. But she couldn't get off that lightly, and Emerald led her through a sequence that actually started to make her feel better. Opal had followed them all as far as the garden door, did a quick temperature check with her tiny pale pink nose, and strutted back into the house again, tail upright like a flagpole.

Once they'd finished the stretches and were sitting down with their coffees and toast on the slightly damp wooden bench, they were quickly reminded not to trust March sunshine as the clouds came over and the temperature plummeted. It wasn't long before Emerald suggested they went back in.

"Just a moment," Tamsin held up her hand to stop Emerald getting up. "Quiz! Where's my jumper?"

Quiz tilted her head and cocked her ears as she took a moment to process the request, then ran back into the house. They could hear her scurrying about downstairs.

"Where did you leave it?" asked Emerald.

"I think it's still on my bed."

"That's hard!"

"I'll help her if she gets stuck .. Hang on! I can hear her thundering up the stairs." She'd slipped her hand in Banjo's collar and parked Moonbeam on her lap so they shouldn't interrupt the search. And in no time, they heard Quiz come down the stairs again - more slowly as she was dragging the jumper between her legs like a lion carrying its kill - and they saw her emerge triumphant into the garden.

By the time the jumper arrived with Tamsin she had to pluck grass and twigs off it, but not before rewarding Quiz with the last piece of buttered toast.

"Do they have ball-boys at this club of yours?" asked Emerald with a grin. "I think there's a job there for the dogs."

Tamsin's laugh was muffled as she pulled her jumper over her head. "Think the balls may get too wet! Here, I have to tell you all about it." She plucked another tiny twig from her hair. "But let's get into the warm first."

Back inside, after casting a glance up at the Malvern Hills - half of which were still missing in the low cloud - and refilling the coffee mugs from the cafetière, Tamsin told her all the gossip.

"So they're all nice except for the treasurer and one player?" Emerald queried.

"That's about it. But you know the thing about bad apples? It's pretty pervasive."

"There's always one ... So will you join?"

"I think I will. There are plenty of really nice people there - some nice kids too. They always make you feel more energetic! And I really enjoyed playing, however badly. Oh, and that means I'll have to fit in a visit to the sports shop in town to buy a racquet before next week."

Emerald gazed out of the window at the swirling mists. "So you already know Julia and Sara. Anyone else you know?"

"Not last night. But apparently Jonathan goes there."

Emerald raised her eyebrows dramatically. "Oh, *really?*"

"Yeah yeah. Enough of that." Tamsin said in mock irritation, and was annoyed to find herself actually blushing. She went to put her mug in the sink to cover her discomfiture. "I wonder if Andrew plays there? He's super-fit."

"Because of Sara, you mean? That would be nice. Haven't seen Andrew for ages. Not since all that mountain biking business. But he's keen on all sports as far as I can tell."

"He's also pretty keen on Sara, as I recall. He's always pedalling, or running, or climbing, or batting ... I'll look out for him. Perhaps he'll turn up when she does, in the holidays." She smiled, thinking fondly of the two youngsters and the fun they'd all had over 'that mountain bike business'. "Now I have to get ready for my first call." Tamsin leafed through some papers beside her laptop on the desk under the stairs. "Ah yes, the first one is to a dog who needs a different way to play since he injured himself racing after a ball. First thing I'll be doing is getting them to bin their ball stick! I was talking about that last night - Julia's Oliver wanted tennis balls to play with Romeo - and I got on my high horse about it."

"You would!"

"It's misery for a dog, being rested for months. They don't understand why, and they can't lie down and read a book! And it's a lazy way of exercising for the owner: no real interaction. Sometimes they're talking on their phones while they wave their beastly sticks around, firing their ball right at other people's dogs. Anyway, that nasty Glenda woman took the opportunity to take a swipe at me over it."

"What's it got to do with her? Does she have a dog?"

"Apparently not. I think it's her default reaction to everything: to be nasty."

"Not a good way to be. She may live to regret that .." said Emerald, winding her long hair over her shoulder.

"Oh, I think she has a thick skin along with her long neck," Tamsin muttered as she gathered her things together.

And then she put tennis clubs out of her mind as she turned all her attention to her first love - helping dogs.

CHAPTER SEVEN

The next day Tamsin was kept busy with home visits, training her own dogs, and her favourite class of the week, her Friday Malvern Puppy Class. She would arrive at her class of six little puppies, thinking, "I can't believe I get paid for this!" Only occasionally, when there was a particularly stroppy new owner who thought they had to bully their dogs - and their teacher too - did she think, "I don't get paid enough for this."

The class was fortunately always held indoors, since the March weather had reverted to type and the rain was lashing down. They'd all got drenched at Banjo's Search & Rescue session on Thursday night - not that he minded!

So it was Saturday morning before she ventured down the hill to the sports shop Gavin had recommended. As she went in, giving herself a shake to get some of the rain off, she was almost overwhelmed by the smell of rubber - presumably from all the shoes. The long narrow shop was crammed. There seemed to be equipment for every kind of sport - football, cricket, tennis, badminton - was that a lacrosse stick on the wall? And there were even some wetsuits dangling from a high rail, looking for all the world like black rubber ghosts dancing above her.

Finding a rack with some racquets displayed, she started to rummage through them, peering especially at their price labels, which gave her a bit of a jolt.

"That's our professional range," said a simpering voice behind her, as if she were looking in the wrong place. Did she look that dumpy and amateur, she wondered, and turned to face the owner of the voice.

He was a young man, slender and lithe, but not very tall, with his fair hair swept up off his face in the latest fashion. He was wearing baggy trousers and a hoodie, to look the sporty part, Tamsin guessed - as opposed to the traditional shop assistant's dark suit - and had his arms folded. Was this the typical sign of aggression? Of closing her out?

He seemed to relent for a moment. "I'm William. How may I help you today? You're looking for a tennis racquet? Is it for a child?"

Tamsin bristled. Who did he think he was? "No. It is *not*. It's for me." She fished in her pocket and brought out a whistle on a lanyard, a tattered screwed-up till receipt, some ancient and rather crumbly dog treats, and the scrap of paper Gavin had given her.

William's lip actually curled with disdain. He held his hand out over hers, and taking the corner of the slip of paper between his finger and thumb, gave it a vigorous shake to remove the biscuity crumbs before peering at it.

"Ah, you're wanting a beginner racquet. Just starting out?" He raised an eyebrow as he studied her.

"Yes, just starting. But I don't know about a 'beginner' racquet. I want one that will do me for a while."

"Naturally, naturally," he cooed. "You're at Great Malvern Tennis Club, of course?"

"No, actually. Their club night is on a Monday and I can't do Mondays."

"So where will you go?" William demanded, and spread out his hands as if she were a waif abandoned in the storm.

"Tom's."

"Oh!" said William flatly.

Tamsin wondered why he should sound so dismayed at this revelation.

"Tom's. Hmm. So you want something that will work on any surface?"

"I believe so ..."

"Let me see your hand. Right or left-handed?" And as he went to snatch up Tamsin's hand, she rubbed it quickly on her trousers to remove any remaining crumbs.

"Hmm, hmm," he mumbled as he measured her hand. "I'd say you're a three."

Tamsin looked at her hand. "Three what?"

"It's the grip size. Very important to have the right grip size," he said over his shoulder as he went to a rack with lots of racquets in. There was a pretty pink and black one - Tamsin hoped she could have that one.

But William pulled out a dark green racquet, flipped it round and held the handle towards her. "Have a go with this?"

Tamsin took hold of the racquet.

"No no," squawked William. "Down here. Hold it down here!" and grasping her wrist he yanked the racquet forward till she could feel the butt of the handle in her hand. "Dearie me, I hope you're having some lessons!" He shook his head in wonder.

Tamsin was finding William very trying, so she decided to deflect his attention onto himself. "You play, do you, William?"

"Oh yes. I play mostly at Great Malvern, but I'm simply *so* busy with tournaments most of the year - being in the top league for the county - I play *all* round the Three Counties."

"That's very impressive. No wonder you're so good at this!"

This blatant flattery seemed to do the trick - to an extent - and he fetched out another racquet for her to try. This one was navy blue, with a flash of light blue.

"You wouldn't have one in pink, would you? Or even red?"

William snatched back the green racquet and passed her the shocking pink and black one she'd spotted. "You're in luck. This one is a three," he sniffed. "It's not as good as the green one, and that's reflected in the price."

Tamsin took the racquet, hoping the cheaper one would work for her.

It fitted her hand perfectly. She tried a couple of swings. It felt wonderful. Smiling, she swung the racquet over her head as if she were serving.

The crash as she hit the shelf bearing tennis shoes brought her up short. Shoes thudded down and landed at her feet. William scowled at her.

"Ah yes!" she smiled ingenuously. "Good point. I'll need tennis shoes too!"

It was a fair while later when William closed the sale and held the door open for her to leave. She felt sure he wouldn't want to be seeing her again. "Ah well, I got what I wanted and he got a sale. All good," she grinned as she pulled up her hood against the rain - now quite heavy - ran to the *Top Dogs* van, and slammed the door behind her. She tucked her purchases behind the passenger seat, got the windscreen wipers going fast, and drove back up to the top road to walk to The Cake Stop.

Charity was already there, with Muffin lying beside a couple of shopping bags. Whatever was in them made a bulge, and apparently it was something soft, as Muffin rested her head peacefully on it. It was unusual for her not to be up on the chair beside Charity, but it seemed that her wet shaggy legs were the problem.

"I can't let her up on the chair till her feet are dry," explained Charity. Tamsin leant over and gave Charity a kiss. "Anyone else here?" she asked.

"Boy Wonder is over there," Charity nodded towards the counter where Feargal was ordering half the food in the café for his lunch. Tamsin rushed over to catch his eye, making coffee-drinking signs. He touched his index finger to his temple in a mock-salute, and she returned to the armchair next to Charity's, wishing that she too had a dog to keep her company.

"I am now the proud owner of a shocking pink tennis racquet," she turned to accept the Cappuccino that Feargal brought over to the table along with his Espresso. "My food is following," he said as he sat.

"Are they sending it via a team of native bearers?" teased Tamsin. "I hope they have at least one elephant to carry it all."

Feargal grinned back. "I have the perfect shape for an active person.

And Kylie is not an elephant!" he added as he received the toasted sand-wich and the colossal slice of cake that Kylie had brought over. As one who appeared effortlessly slim, racing around on her feet all day in the café and cycling to and from work every day, Kylie had no need to take offence. And she didn't. Instead she gave a lop-sided smirk, and spun on her heel, causing her pink hair and her pink ra-ra skirt to dance around.

"So what sort of racquet did you get, dear?" Charity had been fussing over Muffin and not listening.

"A shocking pink one!" grinned Tamsin.

"Like Kylie's hair?" asked Feargal before stuffing half his sambo into his mouth.

"Exactly! There was this weird bloke in the shop. William, he said his name was. He seemed quite put out that I was going to Tom's instead of the town tennis club."

"How odd!" said Charity, bending over to see if Muffin's paws were dry enough. They weren't. So she was condemned to stay on the floor. "You'd think they'd be happy to sell tennis racquets to anybody."

"You would indeed! Wonder what he's got against Tom's?" Tamsin had sudden misgivings.

"Oh, I wouldn't worry, my dear. Probably lost a match there or some-thing. Sour grapes, you know? I always remember as kids, if we lost a race or a game we'd say 'I wasn't playing anyway'."

"Yes! I remember that too!" Tamsin felt a lot brighter.

"Probably says more about him than about the club," said Feargal through a mouthful of toast. Then he swallowed it down and started on his Lemon Drizzle Cake, saying, "No Emerald today?"

Tamsin smiled indulgently at him. "She's probably still stripping the Farmers' Market of all its goodies. That where you've been this morning, Charity?" she added, nodding to the shopping bags.

"It was! And I bought some of the handspun wool from Carmel at *Sheeps' Clothing*. It's from her own Herdwicks - gorgeous shades of grey and white. Look!" She bent to get the wool to show Tamsin, but Muffin was dozing so peacefully, her head cushioned on the soft bag, that she hadn't the heart to move her.

"Never mind - I'll see it when Muffin's out of bed," Tamsin replied.

"Ah, here she is!" Feargal, who'd been watching the street through the plate glass windows, jumped to his feet and fetched another chair, pushing it in beside his own.

"Glad to see she's carrying loads of bags! We'll eat this week!"

"You look a bit bedraggled, my dear," said Charity as Emerald wound her long blonde hair into a rope and wrung the water out of it.

"It's fair tipping down," she smiled, her cheeks rosy from the cold rain. "But I got some lovely grub. Gorgeous leeks, and some little Worcestershire new potatoes from Evesham."

"Goodness, they're early!" exclaimed Charity. "I have to say, I'm happy to wait for the Jersey Royals to arrive. They are quite delicious. Though those do look nice. I think you'll enjoy them."

"Even I know about Jersey Royals!" Feargal joined in, and they had a happy discussion about the contents of Emerald's shopping bags, with local cheese and sourdough brown bread, and some genuine free-range eggs as well.

"That bread and cheese looks perfect for lunch," said Tamsin, admiring the mature Cheddar cheese. "And that means if we head off soon I can actually avoid eating cake for once."

"You foregoing cake? Are you sure you're alright?" Feargal's eyes twinkled as he made a horrified face.

"Got to keep trim for the court, you know," Tamsin grinned. "I owe it to my public."

CHAPTER EIGHT

Tamsin was wearing her new tennis shoes and proudly brandishing her new hot pink racquet in its swish hot pink bag when she arrived at Tom's for the next Wednesday session. The weather had improved and it was a lot busier, so there were new people for Tamsin to meet.

Sara wasn't back from college for a couple more weeks, Easter being late this year, and she wondered if it was coincidence that Andrew wasn't there either. But she was bumped out of this reverie by Julia and Victoria.

"Will you make up a four with us?" said Julia.

"Ooh, new racquet?" Victoria cooed as she peered at the bright pink case Tamsin was carrying.

"Love to! Who's the fourth?" she smiled to Julia, and turning away to Victoria and waving her new purchase, said. "Yes, Victoria, all new!"

"Friend of yours," Julia smiled as she moved aside and Jonathan appeared.

"Hi Tamsin! Haven't seen you for an age. Great to see you here."

"Oh!" exclaimed Tamsin, quite taken by surprise, then gave a broad smile. "Hey Jonathan - how's Teal doing?" She was perturbed as well as annoyed to find herself blushing slightly.

"He's marvellous. I'm doing those things you told me to, and he's getting a bit braver every day."

"That's really good, I'm so pleased. But I hear you're an ace tennis player? I'm afraid you're going to find me a bit of a drag." They turned to walk towards their court.

"Not at all. At Tom's we love to bring people on and encourage them. That's sadly not the case in some clubs. Some people are too full of their own ability."

"I met one of those this week .."

"They are about, I'm afraid .. But playing with better people is a good way to develop your skills." Then he turned to her and said in a lower voice, "Don't worry, we'll enjoy our game."

And he was right. Tamsin had a wonderful time. There was much energy and plenty of laughter on the court as they played. She loved her new racquet and was actually striking the ball rather better this week, though her backhand was still rather more miss than hit.

"Hole in your racquet, Tamsin?" Julia teased, as Tamsin stared behind her at the ball she'd just totally missed. But it was all in good humour.

When they finished their set and handed the court to another four who'd been waiting their turn, she was greeted on the pavilion steps by a tall grey-haired very fit-looking man. He sported a sun tan, and Tamsin guessed he'd been somewhere sunny for his winter holiday.

"Hello - Tamsin ... Kernick, isn't it?" he said as he inclined his head in greeting.

"It is! Are you the Secretary?"

"That's me - Neil Allardyce. I need to get all your details and fix you up with your free coaching session."

"Free coaching session?"

"Yes! You get a Rusty Racquets lesson with Gavin. All newcomers do. Help you with a bit of technique, you know." He smiled kindly at her. "You can fix it up with him direct."

"Terrific! It's a long time since my schooldays - when I last graced the court." Tamsin warmed to Neil, who soon had her logged in to the Tom's system, and relieved her of her membership fee.

"I see you've already met a few other members," said Neil cheerfully. "We're a pretty friendly bunch, by and large .." And at that inopportune moment he was interrupted by a terse exchange from just outside the pavilion.

"It's not too much to ask, that you should pull your weight - ample as it is."

It was clearly Glenda's voice, and the insult was hissed at Amanda. Amanda looked very hurt and hurried away past Toto, who was as ever dancing attendance on Glenda.

Neil grabbed his opportunity to drift away, muttering over his tablet as he was finalising Tamsin's details.

Tamsin turned to find Julia at her elbow. "What's up with Glenda? Did she and Amanda not do well at their competition?"

"Don't ask." Julia started to make a couple of coffees. "Amanda was not on good form. Glenda unhappy." She gave Tamsin a glance heavy with meaning.

"That much I can hear." Tamsin accepted the offered coffee and said, "Pretty busy this evening, eh?"

"It is! It gets busier as the weather improves and the evenings draw out. Don't have to use the lights then. Much better."

Tamsin sipped her coffee and gazed out at the courts. "Who's that playing with Jonathan now?"

"It's Don. He's a doctor."

Tamsin laughed. "It's a case of 'All cats are grey at night'! I know Don well, but not well enough to recognise him in shorts, baggy t-shirt, and backwards baseball cap."

"Oh yes, of course you know him. Wasn't he first on the scene for that poor man they found dead at the river?"

"He was indeed." Tamsin decided to keep quiet about Don's wife Maggie. They were very friendly and enjoyed walking their dogs together. But Maggie was also the police pathologist and had helped Tamsin with one or two investigations in the past. It was best to play down their friendship a little, in case it got back to the wrong ears and Maggie got into trouble.

As if reading her mind, Julia added, "Maggie - that's his wife - comes occasionally in the summer. Oh, there's someone else you may know in that four - the one with a dark pony tail."

Tamsin peered and shook her head. "Can't place her, I'm afraid."

"Oh, maybe she arrived after you'd finished in Bishop's Green. It's Sara's cousin Lucy. She's managing the estate Conference Centre now. She seems to be quite a hit. They're booked out for years ahead, apparently. Quite a few villagers have got part-time work up there at the Manor House as a result. Lucy sometimes brings Felicity along too."

"Sara's mum!"

"That's right. You know quite a lot of us already!"

Tamsin put a hand up to pause Julia as she twisted to look over the side railing of the pavilion. Over towards the toilet block she could see Amanda facing away, her head bowed and her shoulders heaving. Between the sound of the tennis balls being hit and the players' shouts she could just make out some snivelling and sobs.

"I think Glenda really upset Amanda. Do you think someone should go over? I don't know her at all really ..."

"I'm afraid it's not the first time. But Amanda will be playing with Glenda again soon, you'll see."

"A victim needs a bully, just as a bully needs a victim." Tamsin pressed her lips together.

"You put it very well. I think the match on the clay court is just finishing. Ready for another go?"

Tamsin bounced out of her chair, keen for some more play. And on the way they found Victoria talking to Gavin.

"I don't care what she does with her partners - that's their lookout. But I'll not have her disrespecting *me!*" the coach was muttering to her.

Victoria joined the other two.

"More Glenda trouble?" asked Julia.

" 'Fraid so. I'm keeping out of it." Victoria gave herself a shake. "Who's our fourth this time?"

"I thought we might catch Lucy coming off. She's only had one game."

So there were more happy introductions as the bouncy Lucy was pleased to be invited, and turned out to be quite a chatterbox. In between games Tamsin heard all about the developments at Sara's father's Conference Centre and how well it was doing.

"I believe you had a hand in turning Grouse into a well-mannered dog?" she asked, after a scintillating smash to polish off a game.

"He's a nice dog. Just needed a bit of direction."

"Lionel doesn't say much, but I know he appreciates what you did. He likes to take all the credit, of course, but Felicity tells me that secretly he doesn't know how he used to put up with Grouse's hooliganism. *Yours!*" she shouted, as a fast shot from Julia whistled past her.

Tamsin completely missed it.

"Sorry!" called Lucy. "I must pay more attention," and with a sweet smile she made a zipped sign across her mouth, stopped talking and they managed to win their set, much to Tamsin's delight.

Before she left that evening, Tamsin made sure to catch Gavin to fix her coaching session. It was for Friday week morning. Tamsin put it in her calendar, leaving an extra space for a dog walk afterwards and still get back for her Puppy Class.

Maybe she'd see if Maggie was free, as Tom's was so near her home amongst the orchards. She hadn't consulted Maggie for ages - not since the mysterious case of the missing trinkets on Midsummer Hill ... and what followed. They were long overdue for a walk with her lovely old black Labrador, Jez. 'It'll be fun to catch up, without a murder to worry about,' she thought with pleasure.

CHAPTER NINE

Tamsin tossed the phone down onto the table and stretched out her legs. "That'll be nice, guys!" she said to the assembled dogs. "A walk with Maggie and Jez."

Quiz caught the name 'Jez' and waved her tail tentatively, thinking of her old black Labrador friend.

"It's all fixed for next Thursday. We'll go to an orchard. And meanwhile we have work to do!" The dogs all looked alert, hoping to be picked. "Banjo, you have Search and Rescue tonight, so you can pass." Tamsin stroked her grey collie's ears gently. "Moonbeam .. yes! We'll work on your retrieve. It's nearly right. We just have to be sure you can do it in different places now, and with strange objects. Woo-ooo-oo!" she added in a ghostly voice. Moonbeam hopped up onto her lap for a cuddle. "And Quiz?" Quiz waited expectantly, her mouth partly open. "We'll do some more searching work. You like that, don't you!" A big affirmative woof and a waving tail from Quiz!

So she set about working each dog - without letting the others feel left out. One person who *was* left out was Opal. But after lifting her head for a quick glance, and giving her front paw a cursory lick prior to wiping her whiskers, she was happy to doze in a patch of sunlight on the table and let them get on with it.

Tamsin started with Moonbeam's retrieve. It was already very good and smart, and pretty reliable. But she needed a bit more work holding awkward shapes in her mouth, and was still a bit reluctant to pick up anything made of metal. She'd made a lot of headway by getting the dogs to collect and stack the stainless steel dinner bowls each day. And making a big game of it, adding a lot of excitement and speed to 'disguise' the different shapes and textures, Tamsin soon had her little dog racing to grab a bit of hard odd-shaped plastic moulding that she'd found on a walk - but whose purpose was a mystery - a screwed-up ball of chicken wire (very tricky), and finally her heavy bunch of keys.

"Brilliant, Moonbeam!" she cried, as she bedded her and Banjo down with fishskin chews, so they could clean their teeth while they enjoyed a good chewing session.

"Now, Quiz. I'm going to get you to find this old jumper of mine. Hang on!" Tamsin found the unnecessarily long washing label sticking out and tried to rip it off. All she succeeded in doing was to make a nasty groove in her fingers. "Ow! That didn't work. Can you do it for me, Quizzy?" She held out the long label in one hand, pulling the knitted part of the jumper away with the other. Quiz took the label in her jaws. Her eyes lost focus as she concentrated all her efforts on where she was biting.

"Cut!" said Tamsin, "Cut!"

Quiz's jaw muscles tensed and relaxed as she bit, and in short order the label came away in Tamsin's hand, neatly sliced from the little stub still attached to the pullover.

"What a useful dog you are!"

"What's she done now?" said Emerald coming through the back door with a whoosh of cold air, back from her meditation session at the Temple, peeling off her scarf and gloves.

"She's cut this label off for me!"

Emerald peered at the label in one of Tamsin's hands, and the neck of the jumper in the other. "That's amazing. How on earth did you teach her that?"

"I honestly can't remember. I think she just started doing it with her toys and things I didn't want cut, so I simply named what she was doing and now she only does it when I ask her."

Emerald looked baffled. "You named it? And now she only does it when you use the name?"

"Spot on. Dogs are such clever things," Tamsin bent to snuggle Quiz and ruffle her plentiful white mane.

Slowly shaking her head in wonderment, Emerald went to hang up her jacket.

"Here, I'm just going to do a quick search with her with this pully. I'll run upstairs and hide it. You stay there, Quiz."

And after a couple of games of hide and seek, which were very short because Quiz was so efficient, Tamsin was glad to come downstairs again to the glorious scent of fresh coffee. As the friends mulled over the day's events and - as ever - Tamsin thought about her next meal, the phone rang.

"Charity!" exclaimed Tamsin with pleasure as she picked up. "How the devil are you?"

"I'm very well thank you, dear." Tamsin flicked the phone to speaker so Emerald could hear. "I wondered how you were getting on at your new tennis club."

"Charity," Tamsin said firmly, "I know you well enough that that is not remotely why you are ringing. Out with it!"

"Actually I am. You see, I ran into Dorothy today - she's doing ever so well with the dogs. Toffee's really settled in with old Eddie, you know?"

"Delighted to hear it. Go on ... you ran into Dorothy."

"Yes, you see, I'd promised her some of my early rhubarb - you know I grow some in the greenhouse? Oh, perhaps you'd like some. Would you dear?"

Tamsin turned to Emerald and grinned as she made winding motions with her free hand. "That would be lovely, Charity, thank you. So what did Dorothy make of it?"

"She's going to make a rhubarb pie this evening!" There was a pause.

"And?" prompted Tamsin.

"And? Oh! Of course! Yes. You see Dorothy had a visitor - you know she runs a B&B?"

Before Tamsin could open her mouth Charity rattled on, "Of course you do. Yes. Of course. It was you who suggested it to her in the first place."

Tamsin took the phone over to the table and sat down so she could reach her coffee.

Charity's tinny voice carried on from the speaker. "Muffin, bring that to me - oh, it's alright, you can play with that. Now where was I?"

"With Dorothy. And her B&B guest."

"Ah yes, well. He's a traveller - a salesman, you know - making his way across the three counties. And he was staying in Bishops' Green before he arrived in Malvern. It seems your friend Julia is trying her hand at earning some extra money."

"Oh, good for her! I had no idea."

"It's a wonder she can fit another person in that tiny cottage, but it is very charming and I'm sure she's a good cook."

"I think she'd be a very nice landlady."

"Well, Julia came back quite flustered from her tennis practice at Tom's on Friday evening. *She* told *him* - that's the travelling salesman at Dorothy's - she told him that there was trouble brewing at her tennis club and that the Treasurer was on the warpath about some missing sums of money. She said that anyone with any information was to come and tell her."

"Wow," said Tamsin quietly. "No wonder Lesley looked so sour last time I saw her."

"It seems Julia was pretty upset about it. Not just that there was thievery going on, but that she should be asked to provide information. She felt as if the finger was being pointed at her! She felt affronted."

"I can well imagine." Tamsin looked at Emerald who raised her eyebrows and shook her head sadly. "What did Dorothy's fella make of it?"

For a moment Charity's voice was obliterated by raucous purring. "Yes, Sapphire, I love you too. But not now, dear .. " Clearly Charity removed the cat from her lap as she went on, "I think he was amused - a village storm in a teacup. The things countryfolk worry about, sort of thing. But I think he must have liked Julia and he did convey to Dorothy that Julia was far from happy about it."

"That's some great bit of gossip you've picked up there, Charity!"

"Gossip?" Charity's voice was raised in protest through the tiny phone speaker. "It's not gossip at all! It's valuable intelligence."

"You're right, it is."

"Only, you see, dear, I was worried that maybe it isn't as safe a place as I always thought. I was concerned about you getting caught up in these factions."

"That's very sweet of you, Charity. I do appreciate that. But you know what? You've really roused my curiosity now! I have to find out what's going on - and reassure Julia, of course."

Emerald rolled her eyes and laughed. "You just can't leave trouble alone, can you!"

"Oh hello Emerald, my dear!" said the disembodied distorted voice. "You are quite right. Well, don't say you haven't been warned, Tamsin. I felt I ought to tell you."

"Thank you, Charity. You are my guardian angel. I'll be up there on Wednesday to find out what's going on - will you be at the Farmers' Market in town on Saturday?"

"Oh, I will. But I won't be buying rhubarb," Charity chuckled. "See you at Jean-Philippe's then. Cheery-bye!"

CHAPTER TEN

As it happened, Tamsin was not there on Wednesday night for the club night. The rain had started mid-afternoon and never let up.

Tamsin peered through the window at the sodden garden lashed with torrential rain and said, "That's a shame. A monsoon. No tennis tonight. 'You wouldn't leave a milk bottle out in this!' as Charity would say."

"I heard her say that once. What on earth does it mean?" said a perplexed Emerald, who was happily peeling parsnips and chopping leeks.

"Oh child, I forget how young you are," teased Tamsin. "Milk used to be delivered in glass bottles, and left outside your door at, like, five in the morning. Then you'd leave the empty milk bottles out for the milkman to collect the next day."

"They delivered it every day?"

"Yep. Even Sundays." Tamsin leant against the kitchen counter and stroked Opal absently while she gazed into space and remembered back to her childhood. "They drove milk floats - funny little open-sided vehicles which ran on electricity."

"How modern!"

"I suppose they were ahead of their time. They went pretty slowly and made a distinctive whiney noise. You'd hear the whine, then it stopped and you'd hear glass bottles clanking, then more whining as it drove to the next house."

"You were awake at five in the morning?" Emerald tipped all the chopped leeks into a pan and started stirring.

"I only vaguely remember this - I was very young. Maybe I was awake at that hour? Well, it was comforting to hear those familiar sounds, and I'm sure I'd have drifted off to sleep again soon enough." Opal nudged her hand as she'd stopped stroking her. "Sorry Opal. I was down Memory Lane. Tell you something else about milk bottles which I think you'll love!" Tamsin hopped herself up so she was sitting on the worktop with Opal on her lap.

"The milk was pasteurised but not homogenised back in the day. So that meant the cream rose to the top. You'd see a layer of yellow creami-ness above the milk. Now apparently birds can't tolerate milk, but they love cream."

"Figures - lots of energy in fat," muttered Emerald as she added more veg to her pan and kept stirring.

"In the early days there were no lids on the bottles, so Blue Tits and Robins learnt to perch on the top of the bottles at the kitchen door and hoover up the cream."

"No lids?" Emerald looked aghast.

"This was before hygiene was invented," laughed Tamsin. "It wasn't long before then that Florence Nightingale got doctors washing their hands between dissecting cadavers and delivering babies, remember! They did start adding lids made of card, then tinfoil lids, but this didn't foil the birds!" she grinned. "They'd peck a hole through the foil cap and pinch the cream!"

"That's amazing!"

"Some people would leave a brick out for the milko to put on top of the bottles. But most people didn't mind sharing with the little birds. The funny thing is that Blue Tits live in family groups, so they passed this information on to all the other Blue Tits. Some Robins occasionally worked out how to reach the cream, but because they are solitary birds, the fashion never spread to the rest of the Robins. It became a Blue Tit thing."

"What a lovely story! I wonder what they do now for cream?"

"Well, nobody gets doorstep milk any more, and all the milk seems to be homogenised anyway so there's no cream. It's a quaint practice that died out."

"But people feed garden birds more these days, I believe?"

"Yes, I think so. Even we have a couple of fat coconuts hanging from the tree out there - well out of Opal's reach."

"We do our bit for them. I saw Opal staring in frustration at the birds hanging on those coconuts the other day. She was doing that kind of silent quack-quack thing. Funny! Want rice with this?" Emerald scattered some herbs into her pan.

"Ooh yes please. It smells gorgeous! I'll just get this lot fed." Tamsin jumped down and started clattering bowls and dishing out chunks of chicken carcase and sprats to all the quadrupeds.

And so they hunkered down in the living room in front of the fire to enjoy their hearty meal, and Tamsin missed out on her physical jerks for the day.

CHAPTER ELEVEN

The sky had miraculously cleared by the next morning, and everything was fresh and sparkling in the sunlight. Tamsin stretched with a big grunt as she stood up from her laptop to gaze at the Malvern Hills - resplendent in the sunshine - rising up behind their little house in Pippin Lane.

"Hello Hills. Haven't seen you for days. Glad you're still there! I wondered if perhaps they'd rolled you up and put you away till the tourist season begins again." She giggled at the thought. But the Hills looked majestic as ever, and she could just make out a couple of tiny figures walking along the crest of the Worcestershire Beacon.

"We'll have to get ourselves up there again soon, guys - it looks lovely!" She turned to stroke the pair of collie heads that were right by her, when the phone rang.

"Oh, hi Jonathan!" She found herself smiling with contentment as she heard his eager voice. "Cider-making going well?"

"It's going fantastically well, thanks - struggling to keep up with the orders as a matter of fact. Er, I was hoping to run into you last night at Tom's, but, of course, there was no Tom's in that downpour!"

"Yes, I was sorry to miss it. I'm quite hooked. Was there something in particular you wanted?"

"Um, er, well ... you see, it's quite a while since you came over to see Teal, and er, I wondered .."

Tamsin was quite taken by his shyness, but decided to put him out of his misery. "You want some more help with Teal?"

"Yes! That's it! Yes please. Ah, when do you think you could drop by?"

"Well funnily enough, I'm over in your orchards this morning! Maggie and I planned a walk there. How about I come to the house after that?"

"Oh that would be wonderful! Great! I'll see you then - oh, give Maggie my best, won't you?"

"Sure! See you later on - probably around half past twelve."

"Perfect. Lovely. Bye then," and a very perky Jonathan hung up.

Tamsin held onto her phone for a bit while she thought about her cider-making friend. She'd first met him nearly a year ago, over that Farmers' Market contamination business. She'd helped him with his very nervous Springer Spaniel Teal, and found his uncomplicated manner quite appealing. And he was very happy for her and Maggie, who lived near him, to have the run of his many orchards to walk their dogs. "It'll be fun today, fellas!" she addressed her sleeping dogs. "Time to get ourselves up and out. We're going to see Jez!" Suddenly, sleep was banished and the previously calm room was filled with pattering feet and waving tails.

She met up with Maggie at their usual orchard. She was pleased to see her friend and they hugged in greeting. Quiz was also delighted to see her friend Jez, and they touched noses affectionately. The younger Banjo and Moonbeam simply rejoiced in scampering about under the apple trees, as they all set off together up and down the aisles.

"It's all quiet on the body front," Maggie ventured. "Are you slacking?"

Tamsin laughed as she accepted a twig from Moonbeam and tossed it away into the long grass for her to retrieve. "Makes a pleasant change. I'm focussing my energies on learning to play tennis!"

"Ah yes, Don told me he'd seen you mentioned in despatches."

"The Tom's newsletter?"

"That's the one. New Members. And you were there recently weren't you?"

"I was. Had to skip last night because of the weather." Tamsin kicked an old apple for Banjo to chase, her boot spraying water from the grass in a big arc. "I'm hoping the weather will steadily improve from here on out."

"Good luck with that. Remember where we live! It's not the South of France."

"The temperature off the court could do with improving too," Tamsin hinted.

"I think there are always factions in any club. Don says he just enjoys the tennis and keeps out of the politics."

"Wise. You're right, of course. As is Don. But there's one person who seems intent on spreading discontent wherever she goes."

"Sounds as if you're talking about Glenda, the big 'I am'."

"You've come across her?"

"Only at socials. And only to avoid. Don forewarned me," Maggie smiled as she pulled out a poo-bag and cleared up after Jez.

Tamsin frowned.

"Don't look so concerned, Tamsin," Maggie straightened up. "She's just a nuisance. Nothing to worry about."

"I hope you're right. I'm enjoying my new hobby. I've just got a funny feeling ..."

At that moment Banjo and Moonbeam burst into action, hurtling after a hare. Tamsin grabbed the whistle round her neck and gave a great blast. Both dogs skidded and spun round to come back to her.

"That's pretty impressive," said Maggie, as Tamsin fussed over all the dogs, distributing treats to all of them. "I think old Jez might just be able to hear that whistle. Perhaps I should get one just in case?"

Tamsin nodded. "Teach him what it means first - that whistle equals treat. Then blow it *just before* you call his name. He'll soon learn what it means."

"Then he can waddle back to me on his old legs and get yet another treat. I don't want him fat, Tamsin."

"Just feed him slightly less dinner. He looks fine at the moment, don't you, old boy?" She ruffled his neck and gave him another treat, just because. "As long as his neck is soft like this and you can make a good guess at where his ribs are, you're good." She grinned at Maggie as she thought of her pathologist friend not knowing where to find the ribs.

"So I whistle before calling his name, did you say? Why that way round?"

"Dogs are so good at anticipating. It won't take him long to learn that the whistle is always followed by his name, which he knows means 'come'. So he'll anticipate the name and come on the whistle."

"Ah, that makes sense! Thanks, Tamsin."

"Yes. People tend to think that the whistle is magic. It's great for getting the dog to hear at a distance - when they're flying along, ears flapping - but they still have to teach their dog what it means!"

Once Jez had switched from snuffling in the grass with Quiz to plodding behind Maggie, they decided to head back to their cars and end their pleasant walk, promising not to leave it so long before their next meet-up.

"By the way, Tamsin, did you know Jonathan is in Tom's too? You know - owner of this orchard?"

"I did, yes! He was there last week. He's good."

"He's a terrific teacher too. He runs the kids' summer camp each year."

"I can imagine that. Nice fellow," Tamsin smiled secretly as she turned to load her three into the *Top Dogs* van, and they made their goodbyes.

She didn't realise then that she'd be seeing Maggie again much sooner than she'd thought. But rather than for a chatty dog-walk, it would be for her professional opinion as the police pathologist.

CHAPTER TWELVE

Tamsin arrived at Jonathan's a bit later than she expected. She enjoyed driving around the narrow lanes of Herefordshire - seeing the bright green spring growth just emerging in places through the bare hedgerows. As she headed down the long drive into the yard, she noted that Jonathan's farm was all on good dry land, with very few hills.

"Sorry I'm a bit late," she said as she got out of the *Top Dogs* van.

But Jonathan cut short her apologies. "It's given me more time to put together some lunch," he grinned. "Isn't that right, Teal?" he said to his little dog, whose feathered tail wagged fast, though he hung back behind Jonathan's legs.

"Oh, thanks! I'm always hungry," Tamsin replied. She didn't greet Teal - he'd let her know when it was ok to do so.

"I thought we might chat about Teal over lunch. Your dogs ok in the van? Do you want some water for them?"

"They're fine thanks, Jonathan. They have every mod con and they're already dozing. It's not hot - in fact I put Moonbeam's jumper on her before I settled them."

"I imagine she feels the cold, with those little spindly legs," Jonathan smiled as he turned and led the way into the old farmhouse. It had belonged to his parents and he had been brought up there. It had the feel of being lived in for generations. The kitchen had the perfect blend of old and new, with the ancient Aga pumping out heat while the long row of timber windows looking out on the yard, with their square leaded lights, let in plenty of light along one wall. There were new kitchen units in pale green stained wood, showing off the grain, and old beams above the large solid kitchen table complete with nicks and scratches, which had clearly fed many Mapleys down the years. The swirls of the grain gave away that it was made of Elm - that wonderful tree that used to characterise the countryside of Middle England, marching along the hedges, before it was virtually wiped out by Dutch Elm Disease.

Teal had come in with them and went straight to her bed next to the Aga, and curled up to watch them.

Tamsin could see the cosy living room through the doorway where she'd had coffee with Jonathan at Teal's first session. This was a very warm and welcoming house, and became even more so as Jonathan raised the Aga's lid and moved the kettle over to the hotplate. Very soon it started to sing.

"I won't offer cider, I'm afraid," he said, as he poured the coffee. "It's the middle of the day and we're both working."

"Quite so - and driving!" said Tamsin, "although perhaps you're not?"

"As a matter of fact I'm not. My little old Massey Ferguson has sat down on me. I've been tinkering with it all morning and I can't work out what's wrong."

"It's a quaint little thing - I saw you on it once up by the orchard."

"Yeah, it needs to be small to get along the rows between the trees without damaging the branches. It's got to be forty years old if it's a day!"

They enjoyed the meal of bread, cheese and salad in silence for a while. Then Tamsin sprang to attention. "I know! I've got a friend who's really into engines. Loves them. Would you like him to drop over and have a look?"

"That would be helpful. I don't need a modern mechanic with a computer. I need someone who can feel with their hands and - just know."

"I'll get on to him right now," and so saying, Tamsin texted Manic, her hedgehog-saving motorbike mechanic friend who she'd met at the Carol-singing. It was not long before a woof signalled his reply. "He says .. 'A real old Fergie? Love to. Tomorrow afternoon?' There you go - a fellow enthusiast!" With a sudden thought, she texted him back, 'How much do you think you'll charge?' His reply was quick: 'This is the cider guy isn't it? Let me think. Couple of flagons o' scrumpy do me nicely!' She smiled and passed on the message to Jonathan, and they fixed for Manic to drop round the following day.

"So what do you make of Tom's?" asked Jonathan as he finished his large plateful of lunch.

"I'm really enjoying the tennis!"

"There's a 'but' there ..."

"I'd hoped for a nice uncomplicated club where everyone got on. Perhaps that's too much to hope for from a voluntary group. But there are definite undercurrents."

"There are," agreed Jonathan, pouring some more coffee into their mugs. "But I don't think it's anything to worry about. You're a bit fine-tuned to people, aren't you!" His clear blue eyes looked at her closely.

"I do sometimes see things that others don't seem to. Except for Emerald, that is! She's extraordinarily perspicacious."

"She's a lovely person. You go well together. So what's worrying you?"

Tamsin sighed and pushed her empty plate away. "Every time I go there's one person who's making life unpleasant for someone. You know her - thin legs, grey hair, thinks she's the bee's knees .."

"Glenda!"

"Got it in one!"

"She's been there for quite a long time. And yes, she is a bossyboots. But I don't think you need worry about her."

"But she makes people cry! That's bad."

"I didn't know that. Yes, that is bad. Who did she upset?"

"Amanda. But I feel the temperature drop whenever she's around. You'd think she'd notice that she has that effect and .. change things?"

"I don't think she'll ever change, really."

"And then there's Lesley - the Treasurer I believe she is. She seems very frosty."

"She's a dry old stick, that's true. I have some dealings with her over the kids' summer camp. Very strict about me getting my police clearance before I was allowed near the children. She's alright though. Very straight. Like a mama bear when anything is wrong with her precious numbers!"

"She seems to have her heart in the right place, then?"

"I'd say so. What's upset you about her?"

"A travelling salesman who was staying at Julia's, told Dorothy who was his next landlady, who told Charity - you know Charity, of course! - who told me .."

Jonathan's eyes sparkled as he gave a crooked grin. "I see your spy network is in good working order."

Tamsin dimpled her cheeks and carried on, ".. that apparently Lesley is on the warpath about some funds missing from the club."

"Goodness! Who could have done that?"

"You don't think she's made a mistake with her sums?"

"Lesley? No chance."

"Well, Julia was quite upset about the implication that she had something to do with it."

"I don't see how she could. She's not on the committee - she wouldn't have access to any club monies."

"Hmm. Who would?"

"Only the committee, I'd have thought."

"Who are ..?"

"Let me see. Lesley, of course. Then Neil as the Club Secretary. Um - Gavin the coach. Margaret, I believe, fulfils a maternal role - dealing with the children and anyone who needs mothering and reassurance."

"That all?"

"Ah, there's Toto too. Not sure what his role is. But he's been there for so long he's part of the fabric. I know he's always nominating Glenda to be co-opted onto the committee, but there's no chance while Lesley has breath."

"Old enemies?"

"Let's just say, polar opposites. I wonder what this is all about?" Jonathan mused, as he poured the last of the coffee. "Storm in a teacup, probably. Want to take a look at Teal?"

"Oh yes. I notice he's been sleeping peacefully in his bed next to the Aga all this time. Hey Teal!"

Teal looked up and his tail flipped twice. "Up you get Lazybones!" Jonathan chided gently, and Teal joined the party.

From there on they focussed on Jonathan's spaniel, and with the aid of some of the cheese from the table, Tamsin renewed their friendship, and taught Jonathan a few more games he could play with his shy dog that would use Teal's amazing scenting ability and build up his confidence. By the time she came to leave she felt thoroughly relaxed, full of laughter, and at home in the lovely old farmhouse.

CHAPTER THIRTEEN

Friday morning dawned fairly clear, a whitish blob - shrouded in misty wisps of cloud in the pale sky - indicating the existence of the sun, just visible from Tamsin's bedroom window. "Thank goodness!" she told the dogs as she clambered out of bed and gave a big stretch. "I'll be able to have my coaching session, and we can all go for a walk in the orchard again!"

Many tailwags greeted what the dogs assumed was good news. They caught the word 'walk' and were banking on it including them. Quiz's tail thumped the radiator as ever, sending an early morning greeting through the house. Tamsin smiled as she knew this would be waking Emerald and Opal.

And sure enough she had just put the dogs out into the garden and was attending to the kettle and the cafetière when she heard the dot-dot-dot of Opal coming down the stairs, followed by a yawning but ethereal Emerald, who swept her long fair bed-hair back with long fingers and said "Good morning," before yawning again. As she focussed her sleepy eyes, she announced, "You're in your tennis togs."

"I am indeed! Got my Rusty Racquets lesson with coach Gavin today. I'm hoping for a 500% improvement within the hour."

"You sound like one of my yoga students - or indeed one of your own dog students!"

"I'm beginning to feel what it's like on the other side, with people telling you incomprehensible instructions that seem obvious to them. I try to make sure I don't befuddle my students. That's why I never use dog-training jargon." Tamsin smiled as she held a mug of coffee out to her house-mate. "I'll move over so this yowling cat of yours can get fed."

Emerald stretched extravagantly and stepped forward. "Thanks. Here you go, demanding cat," she said as she dished out the food. "I think all jargon is designed to exclude people who aren't in the fold."

"You're right. Trying to blind people with science is an ego-trip for the jargoneer." Tamsin frowned as she wondered if there was such a word. "Opal's enjoying that alright!" she added, as the cat's appreciative purrs as she ate threatened to drown out their conversation. They moved over to the table with their coffees and some breakfast things.

"I don't think I've ever heard you using any incomprehensible words," Emerald said thoughtfully. "What jargon is there for dog training?"

"Oh masses - because what I do is science-based. Let me think ... Negative Reinforcement, Sudden Environmental Change, Positive Punishment, Premack Principle, Relaxation Protocol, The Four Quadrants ..."

"Enough!" Emerald held up her hands in defence at this barrage of baffling terms.

Tamsin laughed. "That's why I don't use 'em! I have to know them and understand them, of course, but then I work out a way to convey them to my students in words that they already use and understand." She chewed a mouthful of oats and raspberries. "I think I do it quite well!" She gave a big grin. "Now I need to get a move on. I'm taking this lot for a walk in the orchards after my session."

"That's nice for you all! I'll be doing a long yoga practice this morning then over to the Buddhist Temple for meditation."

"Amazing place we live in," quipped Tamsin as she cleared away her breakfast and sorted out dogs, leads, and Moonbeam's coat. "Malvern is such a lovely mix of people - scientists, townspeople, hippies ..." She paused to admire her dogs. "Did you know Great Malvern has the highest rate of Ph.D's in the country? Doctorates, you know?"

Emerald shook her head. "I had no idea - but I can see how, seeing as the scientific research facilities are here. Isn't that where they developed infra-red cameras for rescuing people?"

"That's right - one of many things we now take for granted. Like writing onto a tablet or phone."

"They discovered that?" Emerald was impressed.

Tamsin nodded, and it was only when she got to the door that she said, "Oh no! I forgot my racquet!" and raced upstairs to get it.

Emerald shook her head with a smile.

"Don't say it!" threatened Tamsin. "I'm not that much older than you. Come on dogs!" And with Tamsin grasping her hot pink racquet, off they went in a flurry of activity, leaving the house so quiet. Even Opal stopped purring while she had her morning wash.

The coaching session went rather better than she'd expected. Gavin managed to convey his instructions in a way that she actually understood. "Low to high," he said. "Watch the ball onto the racquet," "follow through on your stroke," "I want to see your elbow pointing to me at the end of your shot," "move your feet!" "take the ball in front of you," "Watch the ball! Watch the ball!" he chanted, over and over again.

It was a joy to find that if she silently recited everything he'd said and listened to him repeating it as she played, she actually got a pleasing sound as she hit the ball. Furthermore, the ball tended to land in the right place the other side of the net. This was progress!

And Gavin was full of praise for her when she got it right - so necessary for her to keep trying and not give up. "Great shot!" he called out, "Lovely backhand!"

Tamsin was pleasantly surprised by Gavin. His social manner - a bit smarmy and creepy - completely evaporated as he did what he did best. He was a good player with a good technique, and seemed able to return Tamsin's balls effortlessly, however weirdly they flew through the air and in whatever area of the court it had pleased them to find themselves.

During the session he had become the complete professional, and she found herself changing her opinion of him. 'That's why they keep him here,' she thought to herself. 'I shouldn't have jumped to an opinion without knowing the full picture.' She made a mental note to be less hasty in her judgments. Instinctive responses were all very well, but you need to have the right information in order to form a valid opinion!

As they packed up their gear at the end of the hour, Gavin asked, "So how are you finding Tom's?" with his usual expansive grin, his teeth white in his deeply suntanned face. But his grin looked a bit forced, and looking closer, Tamsin could see a slightly troubled expression in his eyes.

"Oh, I'm loving it!" she replied.

"Good, good." He replied distractedly. "All good. Hmm."

"Are you ok?" Tamsin peered at his face.

"Oh yes, yes! I'm fine. Just got things on my mind, you know." He attempted another toothy grin.

"Nothing wrong at the club is there?" Tamsin enquired hesitantly.

"Goodness me no, not at all. Just some committee business." He gave another big smile and held the court gate open for her. As they walked back towards the pavilion, Tamsin said, "I'll be off then," and indicated the car park. "Thank you very much for that session - I feel I've got a lot to work with now."

"Glad to hear it! You did very well. If you keep at it you'll be able to enter the novice competition in the summer."

"Oh, I don't know about that," she said shyly. "But I hope your committee problems sort themselves out, Gavin," she added.

Gavin gave a tight smile this time and turned to walk away. Tamsin was sure she heard him say "They'd better!" under his breath.

Shrugging this off, she hopped into the *Top Dogs* van and turned the key in the ignition. The dogs had all jumped to attention, tails thumping the sides of the van, giving a cheery percussion performance. "Ready?" she asked, and slid out of the car park.

CHAPTER FOURTEEN

Tamsin, along with Quiz, Banjo, and little Moonbeam, had a most refreshing walk in the orchard. The early spring sunshine dappled through the still-bare branches of the apple trees, the grass was wet from the morning dew and yet it wasn't muddy, and the clarity and freshness of the air promised better weather to come as the year grew older. There was actually warmth in the thin sunshine!

By the time the dogs were slowing down, Tamsin was slowing down too, "After all I've had a tennis lesson as well, you guys!" This didn't take into account that the dogs had covered at least three times as much ground as she had on the walk, and at far greater speed!

So after loading the dogs, taking off their harnesses, drying Moonbeam, and making sure their beds were comfortable and those who wanted it (only Banjo really) had had a drink, she heaved herself rather tiredly into the van again.

"Not far this time. We're going to Jonathan's. Yes, again!" She chattered to the dogs as she drove along the narrow country road, seeing some blackthorn blossom beginning to appear in the hedgerows already. She noted where it was so she could check out the sloe harvest later in the year. There were also brambles in flower. "Let's hope the farmers' hedgewhackers spare them," she muttered. Then, "You can all have a zizz in the van while I see how Manic is getting on with the little tractor."

And in just a few minutes, her van was crunching over the gravel in Jonathan's yard, where she could see Manic's big motor bike parked up already. Even though it was not hot, she automatically found a shady place to park, and adjusted the van windows.

She got out, with her usual "Mind the car!" and wondered where Teal was. He was generally a sharp house dog, raising the alarm whenever a strange vehicle appeared in the yard. Then she heard a spluttering noise from up by one of the barns, followed by a cheer.

She rounded the corner and saw the little red tractor with the bonnet flaps raised, with Manic bent over one side of the engine and Jonathan bent over the other side. The motor was running - albeit rather unevenly - the tractor vibrating and belching smoke skywards from its exhaust, and the two men shouted at each other over the stertorous roar. The Teal riddle was solved as Tamsin spotted him sitting up on the old-fashioned tractor seat - a curved seat made of metal tracery with the worn letters of the tractor's name punched through it, a practical, bottom-shaped seat that didn't hold water and would keep you cool in the summer - for all the world as if the little dog was supervising the operation.

She paused till a few more twiddles with a spanner evened up the engine and toned the noise down a bit, when Teal spotted her and began to bark.

"That sounds promising!" she said, as she walked towards the happy scene.

Manic straightened up and said "Hi Tamsin!" while Jonathan gave a surprised warm smile, and put a hand out to Teal to soothe his little dog's fears.

Despite the cold, Manic was as usual in a sleeveless t-shirt and black motorbike leather trousers. Tattoos covered his wiry but muscular arms, the earrings glinting in his ears under his mop of black hair, his shark's tooth necklace tucked partly into the front of his black shirt to keep it out of the engine.

"Manic is a serious find," Jonathan said, nodding towards him. "Thanks for sending him my way."

"He fixed it?"

Manic interrupted, "Oh no - it was both of us. Jonathan knows a lot about this old girl." He stroked the tractor's bonnet fondly. "I just had an idea ..."

"And it worked! Here, we're about done now. Just got to clear up a bit. Come inside and get clean, Manic. There's a washhouse over here for washing off oil and so on. And you'll stay for a coffee?" He turned to Tamsin with an eager look, "And you too?"

"I've never been known to turn down good coffee!" Tamsin laughed. "Look, I can go in and get the kettle going if you like, while you finish up here ..." Jonathan did like, so - escorted by an eager Teal who still wasn't quite sure Tamsin was safe in the house on her own - she went in to get the coffee started.

She looked out onto the yard through the long row of leaded windows as she filled the big kettle. She could see some of the orchards beyond the old timber farm buildings, and hills rising gently behind them - such a pretty scene. The men seemed to be getting on really well. The tractor fell silent, and Jonathan clapped Manic on the back as they both made for the outdoor washroom.

By the time they'd made themselves presentable and arrived in the kitchen, a cafetière of coffee awaited them, along with a plate of biscuits Tamsin had found when burrowing in the cupboards.

"That's brilliant, Manic! I can't thank you enough - I can't manage without my little Fergie. You must let me know what I owe you."

"A bit o' cider, perhaps?"

"I meant money."

"No - just cider will do. I enjoyed your little tractor - that's a day out for me!"

"Well, that's very decent of you - I'll fetch a couple of flagons before you go."

"There's something else Manic may appreciate?" ventured Tamsin.

Both men looked enquiringly at her.

"Has Manic told you about his hedgehogs, Jonathan?"

"No?" Jonathan turned a questioning face to his new mechanic friend.

Manic looked sheepish. "Oh, I like to rescue hedgehogs," he smiled. "Then when they're better, I take them somewhere safe to release them. Preferably on land without chemicals. Is that what you're thinking, Tamsin?"

She nodded as they both looked to Jonathan.

"Oh! You're welcome to bring hedgehogs here any time you like! I see quite a few around the farm. Gentle little creatures - and in trouble, I hear?"

"Yes, their numbers are decreasing alarmingly fast. Between the roads and the pesticides killing their food sources, they're definitely in trouble. They're listed as 'vulnerable to extinction', and on the international conservation red list."

"I hadn't realised it was that bad," Jonathan looked glum.

"But thank you! I'd love to take you up on that," said Manic eagerly. "They'll be coming out of hibernation any time now, so I'll be looking out for casualties." He grinned at Tamsin and took a bite of his biscuit. "I usually seem to have one or two recuperating at home. I get rid of their parasites, and I have to get weight on them before releasing them. Some are very thin." He shook his head sadly.

"I belong to the latest government sensitive farming enterprise," Jonathan explained. "I remember playing in these orchards as a boy, and I like to think they'll be safe for children to play in in years to come."

Tamsin smiled at him. "That's interesting! Have you talked to Sara about that scheme? She's learning all about this kind of thing at her college, isn't she?" Tamsin turned to Manic and explained, "Sara is a friend of mine who belongs to the same tennis club as Jonathan, so I know he knows her. She's doing some kind of woodland and wetland management course so she can work on her father's estate - over in Bishops' Green."

"I have mentioned it, I seem to remember. And I invited her to ride in my fields too, so I see her on that pretty grey mare of hers from time to time."

"Crystal." Tamsin supplied the name.

"Crystal, that's it."

"Well, isn't this cosy! Hey, weren't you feeding some fruit to that baby hedgehog you had, Manic?"

"Oh yes, they love fruit. Would there be fallen apples in your orchards?"

"I should say! Plenty of them - that's probably why I see so many of the prickly little fellas."

Tamsin smiled as she listened to them chatting about sustainable and toxin-free farming - a pair of enthusiasts. She loved seeing how so many of her friends crossed paths - their lives intertwined in different ways. All with their hearts in the right place. Jonathan accepted Manic for who he was, without being confused by his outward appearance. Tamsin remembered how Manic had explained that he'd developed his butch look as a defence after being bullied as a boy. Jonathan could see clearly the gentle lad behind the disguise.

As they were leaving, Jonathan said to Tamsin, "Hey - why don't you bring your dogs in next time and let them have a run around with Teal as well? He might like that."

Tamsin looked at Teal, who had bounced up from beside the Aga when the people started to move and was now pointing hopefully at the door. "I think I'd start with just one. Wouldn't want to overwhelm the little fellow. Quiz would be perfect - she's so calm and easygoing. Thanks Jonathan! I'll take you up on that."

She drove home with her still snoozy dogs, feeling content and happy. What a lovely life she led! Working with dogs all day and spending time with people with similar sentiments to hers. What a change from the city where she'd grown up! She never wanted to leave this beautiful area in the Heart of England - the Three Counties, with their three Cathedrals. It was the very picture of peace.

Or so she thought.

CHAPTER FIFTEEN

Tamsin and Charity were enjoying luscious creamy cake - a kind of almond sponge cake, with plum jam and cream topping - at The Cake Stop the next morning. It was Saturday, Farmers' Market day. Emerald was showing them up by eating something much healthier while they all compared notes on what they'd bought from the stalls. They'd spent some time plundering the green-and-white-striped-roof stands for their favourite local foodstuffs. Banjo had been chosen to come to the café on this outing, and he suddenly sat up and gave a very quiet 'yip' as the door opened and Feargal's long legs propelled him hastily across to the counter. Muffin opened an eye, saw nothing of interest and laid her head down again.

Feargal turned and waved to the group of his chatting friends, then ran over to offer Banjo his hand to sniff before hopping back into the queue, ready to give Kylie his order for large quantities of food and a coffee.

As ever, Feargal was the very manifestation of a ball of energy - quite unable to keep still - as he pulled up a chair to join them, his red hair flopping forward, unloading his trayful of food onto the table.

"It's just not fair," said Tamsin, in a mock sulk. "You can eat three times what I can, and you're still as thin as a pin."

"A red dishmop," Emerald beamed fondly at her auburn friend.

"I am always on the move, exposing evil-doers and preserving the good," he replied, then crammed half a Cornish pasty into his mouth and started munching. "Anyway," he waved his arm as he chewed, "I'm a growing boy."

"Whatever it is you eat, you look very well on it, young man!" Charity nodded approvingly.

"And!" Feargal swallowed his mouthful of pasty. "Talking of evil-doers, you go over Stretton Grandison way, don't you, Tamsin old thing?" He smirked as she scowled at him at his familiar use of 'old thing'.

"Tom's is over that way, yes. Why?"

"Body's been found - last night," he said, and crammed in another mouthful of pasty.

"Oh no!" chorused Charity and Emerald, while Tamsin leant forward with interest. "Anyone we know?" she asked.

Feargal collected a shred of flaky pastry from the front of his jumper, licked his fingers and said, "Someone found in a ditch .."

"How horrid!" said Emerald.

".. with a tennis ball pushed into their mouth."

There was a stunned silence.

"Who?" said Tamsin urgently. "Who was it?"

"An older woman. Seems she was involved in the tennis club across the ditch. Name of Lesley."

"Ohhh!" gasped Tamsin. "I was right. It wasn't a little thing. Some-one's really killed her."

They all gaped at her.

"Don't tell me you're already on to this?" Feargal paused his fork on its way to plunge into his cake.

"You knew this person?" asked Charity, while Emerald reached out to touch Banjo for a little reassurance.

"She's the Treasurer. Bit frosty, but people seemed to think she was a decent old stick. Apparently," Tamsin leant forward and spoke confidentially, "apparently she was on the warpath about some missing funds from the committee coffers."

Charity jumped in. "Of course! That salesman told us about it." Feargal looked baffled, while Tamsin and Emerald nodded. "But they can't be dealing with large sums of money, surely?"

"You wouldn't think so."

"But perhaps a thief may have a lot to lose if they're discovered?" suggested Emerald.

"Ok!" said Feargal, who'd already almost finished his cake. "So who did it?"

"I have no idea. I was puzzling over it when I heard about it - the missing money, I mean. Presumably only people on the committee would have any knowledge about the club funds? And I've no idea who'd have access to them."

"I don't know much about committees," Emerald put in, as she fondled Banjo's ears.

"I've always steered clear of them!" said Charity. "Too much trouble and argument."

"There's always someone trying to take over the show .." said Tamsin.

"And others wishing they'd never got involved in all the work," added Feargal.

"I can't believe you've lived your long and productive life and managed to avoid being on any committee, Charity!"

"Well, dear, there *was* the Harvest Festival committee. I was stuck with chairing that for a good few years. But I managed to defer always to Millicent Mallard. You see, she thought she was the most important person in the Harvest Festival, and I found it easiest to let her think that while the rest of us got on with the work."

"You managed to keep everyone happy?"

"Eventually I recommended she take the whole thing over. I was better as a foot-soldier, quite honestly. I was glad to hand all the paper-work over to her." Charity grinned impishly. "It also meant I dodged the brickbats from those who were not on the committee and felt they ought to be. Really - you can't do anything right." She smoothed her tweed skirt over her wool-stockinged knees and grinned again. "She made a proper mess of it too! Had to be replaced after another year, but I'd made my getaway by then."

Emerald smiled at this story, then said, "So how could anyone have stolen this money at Tom's?"

"I think we need to do a bit of sniffing!" Tamsin's eyes sparkled at the thought of more investigating.

"Uh-oh." Emerald sighed. "I know that look. I might have guessed."

"Lesley may have been a bit sour, but she served the club for years, I gather. You can't go round killing people and getting away with it," Tamsin sniffed.

"Surely we could let the police deal with it? They must have a lot of information from this ditch where she was found?" Emerald shuddered.

Feargal finished his coffee. "When did you ever know Tamsin to leave the police to deal with it? He gave a short laugh. "I'm sure our Chief Inspector Hawkins gets on his knees each night and beseeches the powers that be to keep Tamsin out of it!" He looked a bit more serious. "It does seem a very curious case. I'm going to do a bit of digging - see what I can find about the club's history, financial status, and so on. Like, does it get any grants from the tennis governing bodies? How does it function? Does it rely on members' subs? Did Tom wotsisname leave any money for them, along with the courts?"

"Wainwright," supplied Charity. "Thomas Wainwright was his name. That sounds like a good start, Feargal." Then she turned and said, "But Tamsin, dear, you've met these people! Tell us about them."

"Ok. But I think I need a refill first. There's a fair bit to tell!" A nod to Kylie for their repeat orders and Tamsin sat back to think for a moment while the barista set to work.

"You are enjoying your coffees today, *n'est-ce pas?*" The familiar deep tones of Jean-Philippe warmed the air as he pulled his tea-towel off his shoulder, balanced a tray on his thigh, and started to clear their table. "You are already solving a new murder?"

"*Bonjour*, Jean-Philippe!" said Tamsin with a look of amazement. "How did you know?"

"Ah!" he said mysteriously, flicking some crumbs down towards Banjo. "You have a particular way of being when you are plotting, *mes amis*. It is clear to see - for those in the know!" He tapped the side of his nose, grinned mischievously, returned the tea towel to his shoulder, and departed with his laden tray.

"Even Jean-Philippe can see what you're up to, Tamsin," said Feargal with a straight face. "You are quite transparent."

"Right then. I've been rumbled. Better start lining up the suspects!"

There was another slight delay while Kylie delivered their coffees and a fresh pot of tea for Charity, and then they all settled down to listen to Tamsin, Feargal bringing out his reporter's notebook and holding his pen expectantly over a new page.

"I don't have all the roles or positions or whatever you call them, but I think I have all the names. The Club Secretary is Neil Allardyce. Tall, grey-haired, polite, very fit. Seems decent."

Feargal jotted down the information.

Tamsin watched till he finished writing, then added, "He's been on holiday. Skiing. Don't know when he arrived back, or even if he has yet."

She thought again. "Then there's Lesley. Poor woman." Tamsin sighed. "Let me see - medium height, thin, dark-haired, silent bordering on brooding. She seemed very sour on the couple of occasions I saw her. But apparently she was a stickler for her figures, and clearly they weren't adding up and she was upset about it. Um, what else? Oh yes, she did *not* like Glenda."

"Glenda?" Feargal's pen was poised over his notebook.

"Cross-patchety player. Thinks she's God's gift to the tennis court. Very self-important. Got a boyfriend - an admirer at least - called Toto."

"Toto?" queried Emerald, as her eyebrows crept up her forehead.

"Yes. Sounds a bit camp, doesn't he, but he seems to be dead keen on Glenda. Despite her being pretty dismissive of everyone, she has a firm fan club. There's another woman called Amanda who partners her in competitions, whom she bosses and belittles."

Charity symbolically wiped her mouth and her hands with her paper serviette, screwed it into a ball and tossed it onto her saucer. "I don't like the sound of her one bit!"

"I think you're right, Charity. But she's not on the committee anyway. Toto is. Not sure what he does - I think he's been there forever. Now ... next .. Margaret. She's the mother hen who clucks about making sure everyone has coffee and tea after the games, and brings dubious cake. I believe she has something to do with the juniors too - she seemed to know them well." She paused while she thought about mentioning Jonathan and the summer camp, and decided against. "I can't imagine her killing anyone." She took a swig of coffee, savoured it, then snapped back to her task.

"Then the last one I know of is Gavin. He's the coach - the one I had a lesson with yesterday. He surprised me. I've only been there five minutes, and I had formed the wrong impression of him. He seems super-creepy most of the time, but I thought he was actually very good as a coach. His instructions are clear, he seems sound technically, and he said all the right things when I managed to hit a ball. Very encouraging!"

"You've gone for coaching already?" asked Feargal.

"No, I'm not made of money!" Tamsin laughed. "This was a free session that all newcomers get."

"He worked hard for no pay, then," Charity observed.

"You're right. Presumably he gets some kind of allowance? He's clearly committed to the club, doing things properly, you know." Tamsin stroked Banjo, who had appeared beside her and whose big grey head was now resting on her knee, his blue eyes gazing into space as he enjoyed being close to her. "Still creepy, though."

"In what way creepy?" asked Emerald.

"Oh, a bit smarmy. What my father would condescendingly refer to as *a ladies' man*," - she put on a snooty voice to say this. "Old-fashioned term for a *gigolo*, I believe. Rather false manner."

Emerald nodded, understanding perfectly.

Feargal drew a line under his jottings and snapped his notebook shut, putting his pen behind his ear. "Then that's our field," he said. "Not obviously very promising."

"Think it's got to be one of them?" Emerald leant forward earnestly. "I mean, couldn't someone else have got upset about Lesley's suggestions of light-fingeredness? You said Julia was offended - didn't you, Charity - but obviously it couldn't be her!"

Feargal cast an appraising eye over his blonde friend. "You could be right, Emerald. You tend to see things we miss. You and your airy-fairy hippie notions!" he ducked as she threatened to give him the back of her hand, smiling the while. Feargal laughed. He knew he was safe: this peace-loving girl would never hit anyone.

"She's right," Charity came to her support. "Unless we can find a genuine reason for someone wanting to kill Lesley, anybody could have been unhinged enough to do it. I'm thinking about that tennis ball. Nasty touch. Was it really something to do with the club or is someone pointing the finger? The police can presumably trace it - don't they have the maker's name printed on them?"

"If they're new, yes," said Tamsin. "But it wears off quite fast. Though I expect Chief Inspector Hawkins has access to all sorts of scientific testing that would find out where the ball's from."

"That's a good point. I'll see if I can find out where that ball came from." He beamed at them all. "My mole is back from holiday. But it looks as though we'll have to broaden the field." Feargal had re-opened his book and was looking intently at his notes, tapping his teeth with his pen.

Emerald sighed. But Tamsin sat up straighter. This was fun! This was what she did best! Tamsin was in the hunt!

Emerald was frowning. "So what did you mean when you said Margaret - it was Margaret, wasn't it? - made dubious cake?"

"Oh, just that we're spoiled here with the Three Furies' amazing creations. Large, luscious, delicious .. " She looked sadly at where her empty plate had been, and recalled for a moment the sweet, voluptuous, creamy experience. "I'm afraid Margaret is better in the thought than in the execution. Though the children seemed happy to tuck into her dry cake." She grimaced.

"It's time we went up to visit the indomitable sisters again," said

Emerald. "I saw Penelope the other day, ordering people about in the supermarket."

"On her own?" queried Charity.

"I thought so. Then I saw Damaris scurrying about after her, trying to steer the trolley. And Electra was off gazing at some scented candles. Away with the fairies!"

"They are amazing, those sisters," smiled Tamsin dreamily. Then she snapped back to her other persona. "Now! Who's going to do what?"

"I'm going to sniff about and find out whatever I can about the club," said Feargal.

"You could look out for those names Tamsin's given you, too," suggested Emerald. Feargal nodded and made a note.

"I'm going to talk to my Hereford niece and find out about Lesley," Charity nodded.

"I didn't know you had a niece in Hereford!" Tamsin stared at her. "Torquay, yes. Hereford - no idea!"

"Well, she's a cousin-in-law technically. Married to my second cousin, Gerrard."

"And is he a Cleveland?"

"No dear. He's my cousin Dot's son, and she married a man called George Henderson. So my cousin-in-law is called Henderson. Tish Henderson, to be precise. Thing is she's something or other in the council, and I know she gets to learn masses about everybody."

"You have spies posted all over the three counties, I do believe," laughed Emerald. Charity smiled primly and adjusted Muffin's position next to her on the armchair.

"I suppose I'll just be a trampoline for Tamsin to bounce her ideas off," sighed Emerald. "I don't know any of these people. But I'll certainly keep my ears open!"

"And I .." said Tamsin, "I will be on full snoop at Tom's. I'll give Julia a ring too. Who else can I ask?" she frowned.

"Sara!" said Emerald. "She must be breaking up soon. She's bound to have some ideas."

"You're right! Know what? I'll drop round to Bishop's Green tomorrow. It's Sunday, so Julia will be home. Want to come, Em?"

"Ok! I haven't been there since all the shenanigans in the village hall that time - you remember, Charity?"

"How could I forget Bishop's Green! After what happened to me there ..." She laid a hand on Muffin for a moment as she remembered the terrible events. "And that thing at the village hall ended up with the police being called. Goodness!"

"Ok, then! We've all got our tasks." Tamsin looked round at them all. "This will be fun!"

Banjo wagged his tail.

CHAPTER SIXTEEN

The quaint village green that gave Bishop's Green its name looked very different at this time of year. The magnificent trees round its edge were as yet bare, and flurries of leaves still blew about, though most of them were by now soggy and squashed into the damp ground. The grass had that neglected winter tufty look, and the little cricket pavilion was closed against the cold March wind.

But efforts had been made: there was a carpet of bluebells around three of the big oaks, and the brave, bright yellow, daffodils at the front of the old, dark green Victorian structure, bobbed and danced in the breeze.

As they pulled up outside no.1 in the little row of five old cottages that had been the centre of such battles, they could hear Julia's Miniature Schnauzer, Romeo, heralding their arrival. Julia's front garden was also bedraggled, but there were already signs of digging and planting for the season ahead. It was the typical cottage garden, with flowers mixed in with vegetables. Last year's runner bean canes were still there, ready to do duty again later in the year.

Julia came to the door, asking Romeo to be quiet. "Who's this!" she was saying to him. His barking ceased and his little tail wagged furiously as he recognised Tamsin and Emerald approaching.

"Come in, come in!" she enthused, and as she stood back for her visitors to pass her in the doorway, she added, "to what do we owe the pleasure?"

"Haven't you heard?" Tamsin turned to face Julia.

"About Lesley?" added Emerald.

"Oh yes, isn't it *awful!* Honestly, I couldn't sleep last night for seeing horrible visions. So I decided to put it out of my mind today. Would you prefer tea or coffee?" she asked, following them into the kitchen and reaching for the kettle.

Coffee was requested all round, and Tamsin played with Romeo while Emerald helped put out mugs.

"No Oliver or Francine today?" she asked.

"Oliver's playing football over at Pixley and Francine had a sleepover at a friend's in Eaton Bishop, the other side of Hereford. Now she's at school in the city, her social circle has spread, geographically!"

"These bishops got around a bit," observed Tamsin wryly as she despatched Romeo to his bed with a toy and came to sit down at the little round kitchen table. "Any news of Sara?"

"Oh yes, she's back from College now! She should be there next Wednesday, I hope. But why not now? I'm sure she'll be glad to see you. I'll give her a buzz."

A few moments later she cast the phone aside and said, "she'll be down soon. Just doing something horsey with Crystal."

"Great! we'll look forward to seeing her again. So ... what do you know of what happened?"

Julia poured the coffee as she gathered her thoughts. "Only what was on the local news. Not much at all. Bet you know more!"

"I don't think I do. Lesley, in a ditch, with a tennis ball in her mouth."

Both Julia and Emerald shuddered together.

"I thought I'd come and talk to you because of what she said to you - about money."

Julia looked aghast. "How did you know?" she demanded. "I haven't told a soul."

Tamsin arched one eyebrow. "We have our methods!" she laughed. "Anyway, tell me what happened. I am agog!"

So Julia explained that she'd been at Tom's one Friday evening, making up a four. "Lesley was there when we came off, and she told us that some club money was apparently missing. The weird thing is that after saying she was determined to find the culprit and have them replace the money, she seemed to single me out. She stared straight at me and said, 'if anyone has any information, they should come and tell me.' I was shocked! It was as if she thought it was *me!*"

"That's weird!" said Emerald.

"So what did you say to her?" asked Tamsin.

"Nothing! Nothing. I was too shocked. I mean, I've no idea who'd want to steal money from the club. But the way she looked at me ..." Julia reached for her coffee mug for comfort.

"Poor you! Maybe she was directing it at the others, but didn't want to look as though she was?"

Julia looked startled. "I wonder .."

"Who else was there?"

"Ah, it was Neil, Lucy, and Margaret."

"Hmm," said Tamsin. "Tell me. Who would have access to the club funds?"

"There's the petty cash box which lives in the pavilion. But it never has much in. It's for tea and coffee and suchlike. Gavin would be responsible for the tennis balls. He must get paid direct by Lesley." Julia shook her head slowly. "I mean he must have *been* paid direct ..."

"And what about committee members? Do they have access to moneys?"

"I'm afraid I don't know. But there can't be much money there anyway." Julia opened her eyes wide and shrugged. "Not enough to make such a fuss about."

"I suppose any thieving is worrying?" suggested Emerald.

"You can drown in an inch of water," said Tamsin, then clarified, "it wouldn't have to be a lot of money for someone to not want it to come out."

"Well yes, of course, that's true. Nasty. But Lesley looked so fierce!"

"Maybe this was just the latest instance of money missing. I gather she was very proud of her numbers and her bookkeeping ability?"

"Oh she was! It was her baby. I wonder ... maybe little bits were going and this was a bigger bit."

"The last straw?" Emerald put her mug down. "I'm trying to work out how anyone could have accessed the club accounts. You'd think only a couple of people - perhaps the Secretary and the Treasurer? Not every-one, anyway."

"How about if someone put in a bill for something they'd done on Tom's' behalf ... but they hadn't done it at all. It was a scam," Tamsin leant forward and put her elbows on the table.

"Possibly, I suppose," said Julia, then she added, "but really you need to talk to someone who's actually on this flaming committee! I really don't know."

"Of course you wouldn't know," soothed Tamsin, fearing Julia may be about to take this the wrong way. "But you *know* these people. Who, on the committee say, would be likely to snaffle something that wasn't theirs?"

Julia hesitated. "That's akin to saying they did the murder!"

"Oh, I don't know." Emerald jumped in. "We're guessing the two things are linked, but maybe they're not. Maybe the murder was for some other reason entirely. It may even have just been an accident!"

Tamsin gazed appreciatively at her house-mate, then said quietly, "It's got to have been connected with the club in some way, otherwise, why the tennis ball?"

"Unless that's a red herring!" said Julia with sudden enthusiasm, seeing a way out of any connection with this mess.

"That is possible." Emerald persisted, "But if there is a connection with the money - it doesn't have to be the same person who half-inched it as did Lesley in."

"You're right. Someone protecting someone else from discovery. Hmm. Who do we have who may do that?"

"There's Glenda and Toto who seem very chummy," said Julia.

"Or Glenda and Amanda," said Tamsin. Emerald opened her mouth to speak, but at that moment Romeo erupted a couple of feet off his bed and raced to the front door with a cascade of barking.

"That'll be Sara!" said Julia excitedly, and followed him to the door.

A moment later a broadly-smiling, rosy-cheeked Sara burst into the kitchen with all the energy a teenager can generate. She peeled off her scarf and said 'Yes please!' as Julia fetched another mug.

There were warm greetings all round. "Haven't seen you for *ages!*" she said as she hugged Tamsin and Emerald. "And I hear you've joined Tom's now, Tamsin!"

"I have. And it looks as though my presence has cast a cloud over the place."

"I heard! Poor old Lesley. Can't say I ever warmed to her. But why on earth would anyone want to kill her?"

"And stuff a tennis ball in her mouth," said Julia, sitting down at the table again.

Sara looked shocked. "Someone was trying to shut her up, then."

"Looks like it," said Tamsin. "Any ideas?"

Sara took a thoughtful sip of her coffee. "I actually hate to think that there's anyone at Tom's who would do such a thing. I mean, it's horrible!"

"But it has happened." Emerald was being very down-to-earth today.

Julia filled Sara in on the money issue.

"I suppose," Sara replied, after listening carefully, "that could sort of account for it. I mean, if someone didn't want to be exposed as a thief. But that's a bit drastic, to say the least!"

"Do you think there's more to it?" suggested Emerald. "That not only were they a thief, but ..."

"But what?" prompted Julia.

"Oh, I don't know. Just a thought .." Emerald trailed off.

"That they had more to lose? Something more damaging to their reputation? I wonder - you may be on to something, Em!" said Tamsin. Then she said slowly, "I'll be there on Wednesday evenings. I actually can't manage any other times. But you two - you've known everyone there for ages, and maybe you play at other times too. Can you keep

your ears open? Nobody needs to know I'm doing a bit of investigating
.."

Sara interrupted her with a laugh, "Then they don't know you!"

Tamsin smiled back. "True! But they *don't* know me. Most of them.
And I know for a fact that anybody I *do* know has clean hands. No
money. No blood."

"Thank you for your confidence in us," Sara leaned towards Julia to
include her.

"Not just you two! There's Don and Maggie, your Andrew .."

Sara snorted into her coffee mug.

".. oh, and Jonathan too."

"*Your* Jonathan?" grinned Sara.

Tamsin found herself blushing once more. *"Touché!"* she said, with
an answering grin, avoiding looking anyone in the eye. In an attempt to
change the subject slightly, she said to Sara, "Have you talked to Jonathan
about sensitive farming? He's really into it, you know, getting the grants
and all that."

Sara relented. "He was talking to me about it over the Christmas
break. Great idea for him, as it fits so well with what he's already doing.
He wants to keep his place really traditional. Organic cider. Love it!
We're learning all about sustainable woodland management this term. It's
so important to turn the clock back to when we worked *with* the land and
not against it." Two pink spots appeared on Sara's cheeks as she talked
passionately about nature.

"Anyway, you're right, Tamsin," agreed Julia. "None of those people
we know could possibly have done anything bad. At least that narrows
the field. We'll keep our ears pinned back, eh, Sara? And we'll relay
anything we learn or think, or even imagine, straight back to you,
Tamsin."

"I'd hate to sit on any evidence or anything at all that could point to
this ghastly person," said Sara firmly.

"Me too!" agreed Julia.

"I find it hard enough to play tennis without looking over my shoulder!" Tamsin grinned.

And, their instructions given and understood, they all fell to chatting about nicer things, including Romeo, Crystal, and all Tamsin and Emerald's dear animals.

CHAPTER SEVENTEEN

"Is Jez ok with cattle?" Tamsin asked Maggie on the phone that evening.

"He's fine. Too old to do much more than plod along these days. What have you got in mind?"

"I thought Castlemorton Common would be nice. Not so hilly as the Hills - obviously!" she laughed. "But usually plenty of cattle. There's a nice herd of Belted Galloways there and a few Highland Cattle with the huge handlebar horns. And sheep - though they may be in-bye lambing right now."

"He's ok with both. What about yours?"

"I'll just bring Quiz, easier to manage just one at a time while we chat."

"We have something to chat about?" teased Maggie. "Now I wonder what that could possibly be?"

"Oh, just friendly chat and banter," Tamsin grinned. She knew that Maggie knew what she wanted, and that it would all be ok.

So they made arrangements to meet the next morning, with Maggie adding cryptically, "I'll just have time to go over my notes before I leave to join you," before putting down the phone.

It was a glorious day on Monday. Castlemorton Common was pretty flat, being part of the Severn valley, and it had a superb vista of the whole sweep of the Malvern Hills, from end to end - all nine miles of them. Today the Hills were a long slate-coloured shape of mounds and dips silhouetted against the bright but pale blue of the sky. It was a view to cherish!

Tamsin and Maggie walked through the brush rather than follow the muddy narrow sheep paths. The scent of the earth was strong! They found an area with fewer cattle, and consequently fewer cow-pats to avoid. The two dogs were quite happy not to avoid them, but fortunately didn't eat them.

"I don't want you getting second-hand worm doses or recycled antibiotics!" Tamsin said to Quiz as she steered her away from a particularly large one. They walked for half an hour, savouring the clear March air and the fresh chill when they were out of the direct sunlight, before Maggie turned to the subject they had both been aware of.

"Bang to the back of the head," she said abruptly. "It seems she was pushed backward and fell into the ditch, catching the base of her skull on a cut branch sticking out at the bottom of the hedge. Tennis ball was pushed into her jaws within, probably, about twenty minutes."

"Not straight away?"

"It could have been straight away, but not after half an hour or so. *Rigor mortis.*"

Tamsin checked the stick that Quiz had presented to her, deemed it safe and tossed it well away from any cow-pats, to land flat safely before Quiz reached it. "So her death may have been an accident? And it could have been done by someone else - the nasty touch, I mean."

"It's possible. Chief Inspector Hawkins is on the case, and he's finding out where the tennis ball may have come from. Unlikely to yield any prints or DNA. But you'll have to do without that information. Not in my remit!"

Tamsin smiled as she thought that Feargal would probably get hold of it from his 'journalistic source' - aka mole - in the police station.

"Two people. Interesting possibility," mused Tamsin. "From what

GAME, SET, AND CATCH!   85

you say it could have been an accident - an argument that went wrong. And then they thought, 'I'll show 'em!' and pushed the ball in."

"Or someone else came along and found her, or perhaps witnessed it, and did it."

"To place the blame? I wonder." They walked on for a number of yards, Jez beginning to slow down. "Thanks, Maggie. It looks as though there's more to this than meets the eye."

"If *you're* involved, there just has to be! I don't know what Hawkins will say when he finds you're a member of this club."

"As are you!" Tamsin reminded her.

"I am. And Don. So that presumably cuts down the list of suspects for him?"

"Or adds one, when he sees my name!" Tamsin laughed. She'd had friendly battles with Chief Inspector Hawkins. She knew he found her very existence aggravating, but he did have reason to thank her on more than one occasion. There were some things that even the best policing would take time to unearth. And Tamsin had a knack of seeing through people.

They were walking in the general direction of the road where they'd left their cars. "You know these people, Maggie. What do you think?"

"Here Jez!" she called before answering, and clipped the lead on her old dog who didn't see so well any more. "There *are* some strange people there, it's true. But however abrasive they are ... murder? Hard to imagine."

"But we have to imagine it. Someone did it." Tamsin pressed the button on her key and the *Top Dogs* van flashed its lights at her. "Even if they did it by accident - they still did it. A sort of hit and run." She loaded Quiz into the back of the van and poured some water for her. "And that tennis ball really shows a lot of venom. Perhaps pent-up feelings, able to release themselves at last." She closed the back doors of the van and turned to face Maggie, who was straightening up with difficulty, having just helped stiff old Jez into the boot of her car.

"You could bring a step to put down for him," said Tamsin. "Save you risking your back. Or you can get nice little ramps too!"

"A ramp sounds like a good idea," said Maggie as she straightened up slowly.

"The trick of the ramp is to lay it flat on the ground and play a game of walking back and forth along it, with a treat or toy at each end."

Maggie nodded with understanding.

"Then," Tamsin went on, "you can raise one end slightly, on a block or a step, until he's happy to go right up it into the car. That way he won't get afraid of the gap under the ramp and think you're leading him to his death." She smiled at Jez, now lying flat out in the back of the car, tired after his long walk.

Maggie shut the boot and walked round to the driver's door. "There's only one thing that can distract you from sleuthing, Tamsin, and that's dogs."

"Dogs' welfare," corrected Tamsin. "You're right. That's me. I can't account for what would happen if anyone pushed one of my dogs into a ditch!"

"Then let's hope they have the sense to steer clear! Hope I've given you some food for thought. It'll all be in the public domain soon enough. You know my hands are tied?"

"You managed to loosen them enough to give me plenty. You definitely can't think of anyone sick enough to do the tennis ball thing? Even if not the other?"

Maggie fiddled with her car key for a moment. "I think you could usefully talk to Glenda," she said vaguely, as she eased her sore back into the car and shut the door. "She was very cutting to Don once. Haven't forgiven her," she smiled.

Tamsin stood thinking for a moment. "Will do. Great walk, thank you - love to Don!" And with a spring in her step she got into her van and followed Maggie off the Common.

CHAPTER EIGHTEEN

"Wotcher up to today, Em old thing?" said Tamsin as she pushed her laptop away from her, flapped her arms to relax them, and gratefully accepted the coffee mug Emerald was handing her.

"Nothing much till my class this evening," Emerald joined her at the table, first shifting Opal along a bit so she could put down her mug, and then scooping up Moonbeam from the chair so she could sit down on it.

"Why don't we drop in on the Furies? Haven't been there for an age."

"Good idea! They always seem to be glad of a break from their super-duper kitchen ..."

".. to drink tea and eat cake in their marvellously antiquated front room!" laughed Tamsin. "Really, it's like something from a tv drama - an Edwardian one, I think ..."

"And such a contrast with the stainless steel wonder where they do their baking!" Emerald nodded.

A while later, when Tamsin was sorting through her tracking articles box and Emerald had gone upstairs to do her yoga practice, the phone rang.

"So how's it going, old thing?" the familiar, very slightly Irish, musical voice came over the phone.

"Listen, you young whippersnapper!" But Tamsin laughed and she couldn't keep it up. She was very fond of her reporter friend, Feargal. "What have you got?"

"Cause of death any good to you?"

Tamsin gave a loud yawn and stroked Banjo's head. "Old news, buddy," then relented. "I had a walk with Maggie yesterday. Did you pick up the bit about the gap between the murder - or accident - and the tennis ball?"

"I heard it may not have been done immediately, but had to be fairly soon after. And I can hear your brain whirring from here. Two people?"

"I think it may well be. Or the person who pushed her over, after panicking a bit at what they'd done, saw their opportunity to insult Lesley. Finally."

"It could be two people together? One did the pushing, and they argued over what to do, and the other did the ball thing?"

"Or two totally separate people. One did the pushing and ran away - maybe without even knowing what they'd done - and the other emerged from the shadows and finished it off."

"This is tricky! What are you thinking?"

"I'm thinking I need to get hold of one Glenda and ask her some questions. She's a very abrasive personality. Maggie's unhappy about her, historically. And last night at my Nether Trotley class, Charity was talking again about the animosity that can grow in and around committees. Glenda certainly bristles with animosity!"

"Where are you going to see her?"

"I don't want to wait till Wednesday night - club night. So - today. Emerald has classes this evening. I can go when Glenda's back from whatever she does in the day."

"Then I think I should keep you company." Feargal spoke firmly. "This Glenda woman, from all accounts, is none too friendly. And if she does happen to be the pusher, or the ball-er, then you shouldn't go alone."

"Ok," said Tamsin quietly. "I've got to find out where she lives first. I think Julia can help me there. I'll let you know when I know."

She ended the call thoughtfully and tossed her phone onto the table amongst the sundry items she had been sorting out for her next scent training session.

There was a large cut rubber band, half a wooden clothes peg, a two-inch square of dark green carpet, a similar square of carpet underlay - brown, and useful for tracking in stubble fields and on plough, as only the dog's nose would be able to find it. There was a spark plug, half a split tennis ball, a house key, and a matchbox - slightly the worse for wear after it was used in a particularly rainy track. Tamsin was always scavenging for useful small objects for training, but they had to be safe in case the dog ingested them - hence the rubber band being cut, so it wouldn't tie the dog's intestines up in knots. She picked out a selection of objects made from different materials and headed out to the garden to hide them. She was careful to walk randomly all over the garden so she wasn't laying a track to each hidden object.

The day was misty and murky and damp, but not actively chucking rain down. After secreting the objects - some in harder-to-find places than others - she came back in for a coffee to let the scent cool a little before taking Banjo out to hunt.

"The dog done good!" she exclaimed an hour later, as Banjo indicated the last of the objects, by stiffening and pointing at the spot. His enthusiasm had been second to none. "I'm really pleased with you, Banjo Bunny!" she said as she threw the collie his beloved frisbee to celebrate.

Peeling off her dampish jacket as she came back in, she checked her phone. Yes! There was a reply from Julia, giving her Glenda's address.

She works in a shop, so should be home this evening. Do tell what you find out! xx

Tamsin looked at the map to see how long the journey would take, then forwarded the address to Feargal, with a suggested time to meet at the end of Glenda's road to discuss tactics. Then she set about the important business of eating lunch.

And so it was that after enjoying lunch, the two housemates set off up the hill to walk to Dodds & Co, the actual business name of the Furies. The three indomitable sisters were so called because their eccentric mother, who had been besotted with all things Ancient Greece, had christened them Penelope, Electra, and Damaris. Once the equally eccentric daughters joined forces to bake delicious cakes, they became known as The Three Furies.

The sisters could not be more different. Penelope, buxom and imperious, was the oldest, and without question the boss. Electra, dark-haired, mysterious, gifted with seeing things, did much of the creative work. Damaris, who resembled nothing so much as a little bird, with her cropped mousey hair and tiny frame, handled a lot of the customer-facing side of the business, and enjoyed escaping from the kitchen to do the deliveries.

It was a steep walk up the Pixie Steps to reach their house. Being on the Eastern side of the Malvern Hills it was always in the shadow long before the sun set majestically behind the Hills. The sky had cleared and a weak silvery light could be seen above the ridge. "It'll be cold tonight!" said Tamsin, as they approached the house. And in this damp, cold, pre-Spring weather, the Victorian house, built from brown Malvern stone, looked more than usually gloomy.

But this daunting exterior belied the happy and warm interior. As Damaris answered the door, the sweet smell of spicy buns wafted out to the two waiting on the doorstep.

"Tamsin!" squeaked Damaris. "Emerald!" She hopped from one bird-like leg to the other. "Penelope! Electra!" she called back down the brown hallway, "We have visitors!"

"How lovely to be greeted with such excitement," said Tamsin, stepping in and beginning to peel off her layers of winter clothing, hat and gloves.

Penelope appeared at the end of the corridor, taking off her overall and removing the net from her hair. "Ah my dears," she said. "You've chosen the perfect time for us to have a tea-break and test our new recipe for Hot Cross Buns. They're just cooling from the oven."

"How wonderful!" enthused Emerald and Tamsin together.

So it was not long before they were seated comfortably in the front room, that room that had been unchanged since Edwardian times. Brown walls, brown heavy velvet curtains, with heavy cotton cream lace drapes behind. There was not a spare inch in the room that was not cluttered with furniture, cabinets, ornaments, pictures, knitting baskets, cuckoo clocks ...

And yet it was a contentedly happy room. Made even more so as little Damaris carried in an outsize tray laden with teapot, cups, saucers, and plates, while Electra followed like a high priestess, bearing aloft a large dish of hot cross buns.

"They smell sensational!" said Tamsin, her mouth already watering at the prospect of tasting them. And they didn't disappoint. The warmth of the spices and their sweetness, their dusky colour, together with the strength of a proper bread dough, made them quite exceptional.

"We'll be looking out for these in The Cake Stop in a few weeks," said Emerald, mopping some melted butter from her chin.

"Good Friday will be upon us soon enough," sighed Penelope. "That's why we were testing them today."

Once the serious business of sampling and commenting on the fare was done, Tamsin tossed in a question.

"Have you three ever been involved in a committee of any kind?" she asked.

The three sisters glanced at each other. Electra sighed and cast her eyes heavenwards. Damaris shook her head sadly. And Penelope said, "Unfortunately, yes."

"Do tell," encouraged Tamsin.

"One of the bakers in the town thought it would be a good idea if we all got together. I really don't know why. We're all in competition, one way or another."

"Though we do tend to have different specialities," said Electra.

"And different markets," added Damaris.

"Well, a few of them thought it was a great idea, and we didn't want to be outside the tent, as it were." Tamsin wondered if Penelope really was making a *risqué* remark .. "So we joined too."

"The Malvern Company of Bakers," said Electra.

"Some company!" snorted Damaris.

"I simply can't tell you," Penelope went on, "how awful the meetings were. One person would have an overblown opinion of himself, while another would just carp and complain. Nothing constructive ever happened. It was most depressing."

"I couldn't get my chocolate ganache right for ages," said Electra sadly, "I was so upset by it all."

"And everyone was getting on everyone else's nerves," added Damaris.

"Is it still going?" asked Emerald.

"Oh no. It folded after just a few months. It seems that the person who'd floated the whole plan was only interested in stealing other people's recipes and ideas."

"My head ached for months," wailed Electra quietly.

"Poor sweetie," Damaris reassured her, patting her arm.

"So you don't rate committees very highly?" Tamsin raised an enquiring eyebrow.

All three sisters chorused, "Absolutely not!"

"Why do you ask, dear?" asked Penelope, as she poured some more tea.

"Ah, there's been this murder, you see, over at the tennis club I just joined."

"Oh yes, we saw that in the *Mercury*. I wondered if you and your young man would be 'on the case'!" Penelope beamed at her use of the modern phrase.

"He's not my young man," said Tamsin, with a sidelong glance at Emerald, "but yes, Feargal's looking into it, for the paper. It all seems to stem from the doings of the club committee. Charity's been telling us about her experiences with such groups, and we wondered if you had any thoughts."

"I wouldn't have anything to do with a committee ever again!" said Electra with deep feeling, pulling her long brown cardigan tightly round her and clamping it with her elbows.

"I'm beginning to think I agree with you!" said Emerald.

"But it doesn't usually come to murder," said Damaris thoughtfully.

"Even the Company of Bakers didn't actually kill anyone!" she giggled. "There must be more to it than that."

"You'd think so!" exclaimed Tamsin. "I mean, it seems that it has to be someone on the committee who's guilty."

"But it doesn't make much sense ..." added Emerald.

"Why does it have to be someone on the committee?" asked Damaris, her eyes wide.

"We-ell ... the person who was killed was the Treasurer. And she was on the warpath about some missing funds. Now, only committee members would have access to any club monies, apparently."

"But was that the reason the poor woman was killed?" asked Electra.

Tamsin frowned. "No, you're right, Electra. I suppose we just don't know. That's what we're assuming."

"Maybe it had nothing to do with the money?" boomed Penelope.

"Maybe that's a red kipper!" volunteered Electra, delighted at talking the lingo.

"You're right!" Tamsin conceded. "Perhaps I was jumping the gun. Perhaps the money is, indeed, a red kipper!"

"So it's back to the drawing board," sighed Emerald.

"But at least we're revitalised with these delicious buns!" Tamsin said, "Oh, thank you, Damaris! I'd love another ..."

And their delightful visit continued, till the sun went down and they trudged home down the hill, in the dark, the frost just beginning to wrap its silvery fingers round the blades of grass crunching beneath their feet.

CHAPTER NINETEEN

A little later, Tamsin called up the stairs, "I'm off out to talk to one of the tennis committee people - want a lift to The Cake Stop for your class?"

"Oh, I'd love that, thanks!" called Emerald gratefully, her head appearing round her door at the top of the stairs. "It's a bit slippery for the bike. I was going to walk. But hey! You're not going alone?" She spoke with concern.

"No. Feargal's going to meet me there. He'll keep her under control!" she beamed. And settling the dogs, who were dozy and content as she'd already given them their evening meal, they set off in the *Top Dogs* van.

So Emerald arrived at The Cake Stop nice and early. "I'll be able to join the students for a coffee before class!" And she bounced out of the van, swinging her yoga bag over her shoulder, and giving Tamsin a broad smile.

Tamsin did a lot of thinking on the way to deepest Herefordshire, and when they met up she hopped into Feargal's car bubbling over with ideas.

"I thought we could say that you'd been asking me about Lesley as you're covering this for the *Malvern Mercury,* and I thought Glenda was the best person to ask as she'd be in the know ... revered senior member of the club and so on. That I was only brand new and I didn't want people to get the wrong idea about Tom's. What do you think?"

"Might work. Can you lay the praise on with a shovel?"

"Oh yes! I can say that Toto said she's one of the most important people in the club .."

"Did he? He may be there, for all we know."

"Uh, alright. I'll say that I'd got the impression from Toto that she's one of the most important people in the club .. I think we need more."

"I could suggest the police are checking the DNA on the ball, and suggest she should be prepared for an official visit?"

"Once we're in, I'd say. Then that might work. Of course she may just turf us out. But I think if we can get in, we'll find out a lot."

"Let's do it!" said Feargal, starting the car and letting in the hand-brake as he slowly pulled out into the road.

With some trepidation at bearding the tigress in her den, Tamsin walked up the path of the ordinary but neat semi-detached with its drab front garden, and rang the doorbell. Feargal stood at her shoulder.

"Hi Glenda!" she said as the front door opened a small amount. "Tamsin, you remember, from Tom's?" she gave an apologetic laugh. "Oh, and this is Feargal. He's a reporter with the *Malvern Mercury* and he was asking me about this awful business and I thought," she rushed on before Glenda could respond, "that you'd be the very best person to talk to about it. So that he got the facts right, you know? I thought it was important that he should get the right information."

Glenda frowned.

"Toto gave me the impression you're one of the most important people in the club. So I thought Feargal should talk to you and not rely on me to give him any details," she laughed nervously again.

"I don't think there's much I can tell you," Glenda gave a little moue at the compliment from Toto.

"Oh, I'm sure your insights would be so valuable. I do think it's important that people get the truth, and not fanciful ideas, don't you?"

Feargal added in his softest, politest, voice, "And the *Mercury* prides itself on the accuracy of its reports. Our Editor won't print anything that isn't thoroughly fact-checked." He smiled disarmingly.

Glenda stepped back and held the door open. "You'd better come in," she said, watching them carefully as she showed them to her front room. The room was barely heated - there was a single bar on the electric fire - the mantelpiece above it covered with little cheap tournament trophies. Beside the small old-fashioned tv was a glass cabinet containing rather grander cups, and there were a number of framed photos dotted about of Glenda in tennis gear - at various ages from about 15 up - clutching one of the prizes. Turning off the television she offered them both a seat, then sat herself, clasped her hands together, and waited.

"Thank you so much for seeing me," Feargal began. "It's about this awful business at Tom's - the Treasurer. Can you tell me anything about her? I'd like to get a picture of the sort of person she was." He pulled out his notebook and pen.

"Oh, er ... Lesley had been at the club for ages. Before I joined. She's keen on figures, so she was the Treasurer."

"Good attention to detail?" Feargal prompted, pen poised.

"Very much so. She accounted for every penny." Glenda sighed.

"You found this irksome?"

"I suppose she was doing her job," Glenda shifted in her chair. "I didn't think too much about it."

"So how did others view Lesley? Was she popular, do you think?"

Glenda paused, then decided on, "I don't think they cared overmuch either way. She did the work she was elected to do. Played a bit of mediocre tennis. She wasn't what you might call the life and soul of the party." She fingered her blanket which she'd cast aside when they'd arrived.

"And had anything unusual happened recently, Glenda? Anything that might have triggered an attack?"

"How would I know?" she snorted. "I don't join in with gossip at the club. I'm focussed on my tennis."

Completely unruffled, Feargal went on, "You doubtless heard about the tennis ball?" He rose an enquiring eyebrow, then said, "It seems a very pointed gesture."

"That whoever did it didn't like her? I'd have thought that much was obvious." She shrugged and drew the blanket over her cold knees.

"The police are very interested in that tennis ball," put in Tamsin, pulling her coat tighter around her. "*Apparently,*" she leant forward eagerly, "they can tell where it came from and who'd handled it! They're so clever, with all their tests .."

This had more than the desired effect on Glenda. She blanched, then coughed, then shifted in her chair again. She looked about her then burst out, "Well, if it came from Tom's, anybody could have handled it! Unless it was brand new. Was it a brand new ball?" She stared accusingly at Feargal.

"That I can't tell you," Feargal smiled, "I don't know."

"They can't tell much from the ball!" Glenda insisted.

"So whoever added that touch will go undetected, you mean?"

"Oh. No. No. Of course not." Glenda looked very uncomfortable. "I mean people can't go around doing things like that .. killing someone and sticking a ball in their mouth."

"It does suggest that they were shutting her up, doesn't it?"

Glenda was silent for a bit, while she fiddled absently with a broken fingernail, then smoothed the blanket again. "I don't know what the police are doing. But perhaps you, young man, could perform a service by finding out who stood to gain from our Treasurer's death. Isn't that always the top suspect?"

"That's a very good point!" Feargal mumbled as he made a note in his book, "*Who stood .. to .. gain ...*". Then he looked up and said, "So who did stand to gain?"

"I have no idea! Presumably whoever shut her up had something they wanted kept secret. Seems obvious to me ..."

"So what sort of secrets would Lesley have held?"

There was a pause. Tamsin decided to jump in and steer the conversation a little. "I heard she was unhappy about some money having gone missing from the club accounts. Is that what you mean, Glenda?"

"I believe that was so. But I don't know who would have access to the club accounts. Presumably someone on the committee." She sniffed, held up her chin and said, "*I'm* not on the committee," folded her arms and leant back in her chair.

"You're far too busy playing brilliant tennis!" exclaimed Tamsin, indicating the trophies and the photographs. "Who's that with you in that photo?"

"That one? That was the club championships. Toto played mixed with me." Her face softened. "It's the third time we've won it."

"I'm surprised they haven't snaffled you for the committee!" said Feargal. "They like dedicated people, don't they, and you have certainly shown that."

This blatant sycophancy was accepted by Glenda as her due. She basked in it. "Toto has put my name forward a few times, but they've chosen not to elect me." She held her chin up again.

"They'll have a vacancy now!" said Tamsin cheekily. "Could be your moment ..."

Glenda turned and looked her in the eye. "I hadn't thought of that. As I said, I'd rather *play* tennis than *organise* it."

Feargal flipped back a page in his notebook. "So you think someone on the committee may have something to do with this?"

"Of course I don't think that! You're putting words into my mouth! You're not going to go misquoting me are you?" She sat up straight in her chair. "I'll be on to your Editor in a flash if that's the case." She glowered at him.

"Ah no, I won't be quoting you at all. No names, no pack-drill," he winked. "But I would be interested to know who you think I should talk to next, who I may learn from?"

Glenda chewed her lip for a moment, caught in indecision. She stood up abruptly, dropping the blanket to the floor again, and Feargal and Tamsin stood as well. She started to walk to the door then stopped and said, without looking at them, "You may find Gavin has something to say."

She pulled open the front door.

Feargal turned and gave a slight bow. "Thank you so much. You've been most helpful."

For a moment Glenda's eyes widened with alarm - for she had not intended to be in the least helpful. "No names, remember?"

"No names!" Feargal smiled and ushered Tamsin out before him, into the chilly night.

CHAPTER TWENTY

Tamsin and Feargal got into his car in silence and drove back to where Tamsin had left hers at the top of the road.

"Well!" she said, as the car stopped. "She was quick enough to drop Gavin in it!"

"The whole committee really."

"Do you think Gavin is the guilty party?"

"I think she was squirming. Desperate to appear helpful while not actually telling us anything. I bet she's on the blower to Toto right now."

"Interesting - how she reacted to the ball DNA thing!"

"Most interesting. Was she protecting herself, or someone else?" Feargal arched an eyebrow as he looked quizzically at Tamsin, who said, "I wonder where Gavin lives. It's not late. How about we pull the same trick with him?"

"I'm up for that! How can you get his address?"

"Same as before," said Tamsin, already tapping into her phone. "I'm asking Julia." She sent her text, and as they waited, Tamsin started to poke about in the pocket of Feargal's door.

"What have you been up to here?" she demanded, holding up first several empty chocolate wrappers, then a bag with a few sweets that had gone sticky on some far-off sunny day ("Eeuuh"), and a couple of parking tickets.

"Just the detritus of the busy life of an investigative reporter," he grinned. "I clear it out every year or two."

Tamsin's phone buzzed and she stuffed the parking tickets back in the door pocket. "It's not that far away, look," she showed him the text.

Feargal tapped the details into his satnav then pulled out into the road. "We can come back for your car after."

Gavin's house was an altogether more desirable place than Glenda's. Even in the dark they could see that it was a large detached house, with twinkling lights at the front. They crunched up the gravelled drive through the well-cultivated and neat front garden and rang the bell, which played a jingly tune inside.

The warmth from the house wafted out to greet them as the front door was pulled open. Gavin's face turned from puzzlement to recognition as he saw Tamsin, then more puzzlement as he saw Feargal at her shoulder. "Ah, Tamsin! Everything all right? Have you brought us a potential new player?"

"Hi Gavin, this is Feargal - friend of mine. Sorry to butt in on you unannounced, but we were out this way, you see, and Feargal actually works for the *Malvern Mercury* and he's been asking me about this awful business with Lesley," she ran on breathlessly. "And *I thought* .. really he'd be better talking to someone who knew what it was all about rather than me just guessing."

Feargal said, "Good evening, Gavin," in his very best quiet voice.

"That would all be very well if I *did* know what it was all about!" Gavin barked out a laugh and showed all his white teeth. "But I'm pretty much in the dark. Dreadful business," he nodded vigorously, setting his face again.

Feargal stepped forward. "What I was hoping to learn was a little about the poor lady, so I could write something decent about her. You know how people tend to go 'no smoke without a fire'? It would be unfortunate if some other paper were to get in first and sow that idea in people's minds, don't you agree? It could show Tom's in a very bad light ..."

Gavin let go of the door and ushered them in. "You'd better come in."

Gavin's living room was positively palatial compared with the one they'd just left. The furnishings oozed comfort and warmth, the soft lighting from the lamps on the occasional tables giving the room a warm glow, echoed by the crackling fire in the hearth. There was a large flatscreen tv over the fireplace. Like Glenda, Gavin had some tennis photos on display, but his were in a small grouping over a bureau, and were clearly taken at important events. Tamsin could recognise the distinctive green and purple colours of Wimbledon in one where Gavin, clad in white, shook hands with a suited dignitary as they both beamed at the camera.

"What a lovely room!" exclaimed Tamsin, peeling off her coat, and putting it beside her on the sofa as she sat down. She moved aside the book that Gavin had presumably been reading, a ghosted and revealing autobiography from one of the top tennis stars.

Like Glenda, Gavin was reluctant to offer any hospitality, hoping to keep the meeting short. He sat in an armchair, his fingers drumming on the arms. "So what is it you'd like to know?"

"What I really want to know," Feargal said slowly, "is what sort of person Lesley was."

"You're not trying to find out who did this awful thing, are you?"

"Oh no!" said Feargal quickly, and would have crossed his fingers if they'd been behind his back. "All that kind of thing's best left to the police. No, I want to get a picture of her - what she was like, what Tom's meant to her - that kind of thing."

So Gavin relaxed a little and started to tell Feargal what he knew of Lesley. How she'd been involved in the club for ever, had always gone the extra mile for Tom's, and relished her position as Treasurer.

"Was she good at it?"

"Oh yes - very efficient. Scrupulous with the club's accounts. I don't think anyone had any complaints about her work there."

"What about the suggestion of pilfering?" burst in Tamsin. "That must have put some people's backs up?"

Gavin paled beneath his mahogany tan, then blustered, "Well, I think maybe she'd got it wrong, you know. Lost a page of her spreadsheet and panicked, don't you know?" he guffawed for a moment, cleared his throat and became silent.

"She did seem to think there was money missing, though, didn't she," Tamsin replied coolly into the silence. "It may not have been much, but I suppose it was the principle of the thing .."

"The timing of her unfortunate death just after she'd been making these enquiries does seem to link the two things," added Feargal. "But you think her fears were unfounded?"

Gavin looked relieved at the straw Feargal had offered him to clutch at. "Most definitely. Nothing like that at Tom's, I can assure you!"

Feargal tapped his pen against his lips for a moment as he looked down at his notebook. "Other than that, was Lesley popular?"

"Not exactly *popular*, more a part of the fabric, I'd say."

"She could be a bit challenging?"

A log spat and Gavin looked into the flames of the fire. "She was a decent person, doing her best. Loved tennis .."

Tamsin leant forward, "Only - you know about the tennis ball? That was a pretty nasty thing to do, don't you think? It suggests someone wanted to shut her up?"

"I incline more to the view that some tramp or mugger knocked her over, then seeing that they were near the tennis club, tried to deflect the blame onto Tom's. That's it," he nodded. "That'll be what happened." And he settled back into his armchair again, as if the matter were closed.

"The police are testing the tennis ball for DNA and whatnot. They'll be seeing if they can match it to the balls they'll find in the pavilion. Do you think it came from there?"

Gavin paused, frowning. "You were there, Tamsin, when the children were finding lost tennis balls in the hedge. There could easily be some lying about in the hedge outside the club. Tramp probably picked it up there." He crossed his legs as well as his arms, in a closing gesture.

"It's true that it could have been a completely random attack," conceded Feargal, "but I do believe the police are regarding it as a deliberate act."

"You know how they say that the cause of someone being killed is in something they did, or what they represent?" added Tamsin.

"That's the view they're taking, anyway," Feargal continued.

Tamsin thought for a moment as they all watched another log crack in the grate, a spurt of flame dancing as the fire collapsed slightly. "If she did think that someone had taken something they shouldn't have, then wouldn't that be a reason for someone to want to shut her up?"

"Hence the tennis ball in her mouth?" added Feargal.

"*If* that were the case, then I suppose someone may have something to hide. But I really can't accept that anyone involved with Tom's - least of all the committee - had anything to do with such an appalling thing." He uncrossed his legs and crossed them again, uncrossed his arms then clasped his hands across his ample belly.

"Tell me, Gavin - how long have you been at Tom's?"

"Oh, years, on and off. But I was appointed Head Coach - let me see ... about four years ago."

"Tamsin tells me you're an excellent coach!"

"Thank you, m'dear," he inclined his head towards Tamsin, relaxing his hands again.

"And would you say it's a happy club? No grievances or complaints?"

Gavin spread out his hands. "Not that I know of." He thought for a moment, then burst out, "Now even if that ball .. that ball .. even if it was put in her mouth ..." he shuddered rather over-dramatically. "No. No-one at Tom's would do a thing like that."

"Thank you for being so forthcoming with me, Gavin," said Feargal, snapping shut his notebook.

Gavin stood up. "Oh, not at all, not at all, my dear fellow. Just you make sure you don't print anything that I didn't say. And, er, actually, I'd rather you didn't attribute anything to me, know what I mean?" He leant forward to stare at Feargal.

"I should be able to manage that. 'Source close to the club' kind of thing." He smiled reassuringly, in a man-to-man way.

They all made their way to the door, Tamsin slipping on her jacket again. Then she turned and said, "Gavin, who do you think may know more about this? I mean, perhaps someone who was close to Lesley? Or someone who was upset about the suggestions of pilfering?"

Gavin blustered.

"How about Neil? Do you think he could tell us more?"

"Yes, yes, capital fellow Neil. Do talk to him." He edged them closer to the door.

But Tamsin wasn't done yet. "Margaret's been at Tom's for ages, hasn't she?"

Gavin looked trapped, in his own doorway. "I don't think she'd have very much to contribute," he said stiffly. "Waste of your time, you know."

At which Tamsin and Feargal re-iterated their goodbyes and slipped out into the cold night air.

CHAPTER TWENTY-ONE

Having done all they could on Tuesday evening, Tamsin and Feargal agreed to meet up at their favourite café on Wednesday morning.

"*Bonjour, Mademoiselle* Tamsin! And *Mademoiselle* Emerald!" said a deep, cheery voice as the two housemates came in to The Cake Stop with Moonbeam trotting between them.

"*Bonjour, Monsieur Jean-Philippe!*" Tamsin replied equally cheerily, as Emerald smiled sweetly, and they made their way to the counter, Tamsin keeping her eyes firmly away from the cake display.

"I think you are avoiding the Furies' splendid *gateaux,*" Jean-Philippe protested.

Tamsin patted her tummy. "In training!" she said with a grin, offering Kylie her card for her luscious calorie-laden coffee.

"In training for tennis?" Jean-Philippe arched a bushy black eyebrow. "Or for capturing *les méchants?*" His dark brown eyes peered at her, with a glint of humour.

Tamsin laughed. "You got me! I'm keeping my brain sugar-free for the morning's deliberations." She leant towards Jean-Philippe and stage-whispered, "We're having a council of war," then made a bee-line for the armchairs in the front window which were fortunately free, set down a mat for Moonbeam and sat herself down with a sigh and a smile to Emerald.

It wasn't long before the door burst open and in swept Feargal, always in a hurry. But he stopped, spun round, and held the door open for the diminutive figure of Charity.

"Thank you, my dear," she said as she turned to the little fluffy dog following her. "Come along, Muffmuff!"

"Look who I found on the top road!" Feargal beamed as he ushered Charity over to the third armchair that Tamsin had pulled up to the table. "Tea for you?"

"That would be lovely, dear! And you'd better fetch over that other armchair for yourself."

Feargal pushed another armchair up to the table, as close as he could get it to Emerald's, and strode to the counter to put the world to rights with Kylie.

"I was just walking down towards *Malvhina*, you know, the well by Elgar," Charity referenced the spring next to the statue right in the centre of town - of Malvern's most famous son, the composer Sir Edward Elgar of *Land of Hope and Glory* fame, and its nearby much-decorated water-spout - one of so many springs on the Malvern Hills. "And who should I see charging along the top road but young Feargal. He tells me you've both been investigating ... I'm all ears!" She wiggled her shoulders dramatically.

"Charity - you're as bad as me! You can't keep your nose out of a mystery," giggled Tamsin. "Let's wait for the intrepid reporter to join us."

So they diverted themselves by settling Muffin and Moonbeam - already firm friends - together on Moonbeam's mat, with a fishskin chew each to keep them amused. Tamsin smiled as she remembered how Moonbeam, even as a tiny puppy, would snarl at the other dogs when she was eating. A little reassurance and confidence-building had been all it took to allow her to lie down now beside Muffin to eat their chews in companionable silence. Her apparent aggression had simply been fear that she'd lose her food.

When Feargal arrived at the table with a tray bearing Charity's pot of tea and his coffee, he also unloaded plates of food for himself. Tamsin shifted in her seat to avert her gaze, hoping she wouldn't embarrass herself by drooling like a Labrador at the sight of a biscuit.

"Tell us all about last night?" said Emerald impatiently.

"Interesting." The thin reporter took a large bite of his toasted panini and chewed thoughtfully.

Tamsin jumped into the breach. "We went to see Glenda, the star player, and she sent us to see Gavin - the coach," she explained to Charity as Feargal munched his way through his first plateful of food. "And you won't be surprised to know that there are plenty of undercurrents in the calm sea that is Tom's Tennis Club."

Charity sighed. "There always are. Why people can't just get along and keep their club or society going without it being all about themselves, I really don't know."

"It seems Glenda is totally devoted to her tennis. She seems to have no home comforts. Her house was cold!"

"To go with her frosty nature, perhaps?" Feargal pushed away the first empty plate and reached for the next, full, one.

"I have to say she looked shocked when I suggested the police would be able to trace the ball and who'd handled it!"

"Can they really?" asked Emerald.

"I've no idea. I only suggested it!" Tamsin grinned.

"That could be a sign of guilt," mused Charity. "But it could also be that she suspects someone else ..."

"And doesn't want them found! Charity, you could be right."

Feargal, with his mouth full, nodded vigorously. And eventually swallowing, said, "That's kinda the impression I got."

"Other than that we didn't get much from our Glenda," Tamsin said, turning to fondle Moonbeam's massive ears, the little dog having transferred herself unobserved to Emerald's lap.

"But she was very scathing about - well, everybody really," Feargal added. By now he'd polished off two plates of food and was ready to rejoin the human race and engage in the conversation again. "Anyhow, she told us to talk to Gavin, the coach. Which we did."

"He seems in a far better emotional place than Glenda," said Tamsin. "Warm, comfortable home - presumably got a decent job to cover it. Wonder what he does for a living? Obviously very keen on tennis, but he seemed much more balanced, don't you think, Feargal?"

"I do. He was keen for us to talk to Neil, the Secretary."

"But very much didn't want us to talk to Margaret!" put in Tamsin quickly.

"Which means that you know exactly who to talk to next!" Charity grinned.

"Exactly," Tamsin replied, with a smirk.

"I wonder why he doesn't want you to talk to Margaret?" asked Emerald, winding a strand of her long blonde hair round an elegant finger.

"I believe she's been at Tom's for a long time," said Tamsin. "I got the idea she was part of the fabric."

"Is she a committee member?" asked Charity.

"She is. I gather she's involved with the kids' camp in the summer. She's a mother hen. Always fussing about and making sure everyone has tea and dull cake and so on."

"Ah, the summer camp that Jonathan takes .." said Emerald, provokingly.

"That summer camp, yes." Tamsin said with finality. Emerald and Feargal exchanged a grin.

"Maybe Lesley cramped her style in some way?" said Charity, letting Emerald's teasing pass, though she was dying to find out what it was about!

"Or maybe she's been cooking the books as well as cakes .." suggested Emerald.

".. and needed to hush Lesley up!" said Feargal, giving her a broad smile.

"Yes," said Tamsin slowly, "she'd presumably have access to club funds, for what she does. We need to talk to her today. She's always early - I'll get there ahead of time tonight and have a chat."

They all thought for a moment as they finished their drinks and

Charity invited Muffin onto her chair with her, "Up you jump, Muffy-moo!"

"Hey Charity! Did you find anything out from your step-cousin-in-law-twice-removed - the one in the Council?" Tamsin suddenly remembered what Charity had said at their previous meeting.

"Tish Henderson? Yes, I did speak to her. And she was most interesting. It seems Lesley was pretty vocal in defence of her club. Tish had come across her when she was in Parks and Recreation, when Lesley was looking for funds for Tom's. And then she campaigned for the improvement to the road outside the club, to make it easier for players to park. Tragically, it seems the maintenance of that hedge and ditch were down to her efforts."

They all paused for a moment. "How very sad. And for all this campaigning .. did they think her a nuisance?"

"I had the impression that it was all pretty businesslike. No problems. But Lesley couldn't be fobbed off. She was very determined."

Feargal sighed. "It seems that her very determination - to do right by the club - may have been her downfall." And he put his empty mug on his pile of empty plates and swished his hands against each other to swipe off the crumbs.

CHAPTER TWENTY-TWO

Tamsin made sure to roll up to Tom's a good half-hour early that evening. It was dark long since, but she could smell the young growth in the moist earth below the hedgerow, with its promise of a warm summer to come. And she didn't have to wait long by the road before Margaret turned up in her old banger. Tamsin jumped out and was ready with her pink racquet as Margaret got out of her car.

"I had to see someone in Ledbury," Tamsin explained, "so I came straight here. I'm awfully early! I'm glad you've arrived." She noticed that Margaret's ample posterior was sticking out of one of the rear doors of the car. "Oh, can I help you with anything, Margaret?"

"Yes please, dearie - I've made lots of jam tarts for this evening." She handed a plastic container to Tamsin, and said quietly, "I think everyone will need cheering up. There's some gingerbread too." She heaved out a big bag along with her tennis bag and straightened up. "I haven't been here since .. since .." and she stared at the hedge and ditch to the left of the club gates.

Tamsin followed her gaze. "Is that where .. I mean, that awful thing happened?"

"Right there." Margaret nodded her head towards a trampled area of grass. "They said it in the papers, that's how I know!" she added quickly. "And I drove past on Monday and the blue and white police tape was still there."

"Gone now," said Tamsin, making a move towards the gate and waiting for Margaret to produce a key. "Let's get these in to the pavilion." But Margaret didn't need to find a key. She put down her burden and fiddled with the combination lock till the padlock pinged open.

That's interesting, thought Tamsin. Anyone could know the combination. Anyone could go in and tamper with the tennis balls .. She followed Margaret through the gate and pulled it to behind her. "So tell me, Margaret, how *did* you hear about it - what happened to Lesley, I mean?"

Margaret fiddled with yet another padlock, this time on the pavilion door, and said distractedly, "Oh, Gavin rang me. I think he was ringing everyone, not just me."

"How did he know?" Tamsin asked idly, picking up Margaret's racquet and tucking it under her arm with her own, while balancing the box of tarts in her other hand.

"No idea. I suppose the police needed to get in touch with someone from the club, and found Gavin." And she led the way into the pavilion.

Tamsin followed her, and they put their loads onto the table by the kettle. Margaret started to bustle about, filling the kettle, setting out the teacups and mugs, getting milk from her box and decanting some into a milk jug.

"It'll be a huge loss," Tamsin tried again to get something from Margaret. "I mean, she must have been a big part of the club."

"Too big, some would say," Margaret re-adjusted her shoulders in a dismissive gesture and carried on filling the sugar bowl.

"She wasn't loved?"

"Lesley," said Margaret solemnly as she turned to face Tamsin, "was not the lovable type. She was the sort of person who had to seek validation by being useful."

Ouch! thought Tamsin. "Not naturally attractive?" she ventured.

"Not attractive in any way."

"That must have been hard for you, being on the committee and having to work with her?"

In her most martyred voice Margaret sighed, "These things are sent to try us," then straightened a couple of mugs.

"Will she be hard to replace? I heard she was very hot on her figures!"

"That'll be for Neil to decide."

"Oh, is Neil back from holiday?"

"Yes, over the weekend, I believe," she answered abstractedly. "It's not as if Tom's handles much money - I think she just went on about it to make herself more important." Margaret suddenly seemed to remember herself and switched to the persona Tamsin had got used to. "Would you like a drink now, before everyone else arrives, Tamsin?"

"Oh thank you - yes, that would be nice. I'll do it. Shall I make one for you too?" And she set about busying herself with making two cups of tea. She'd always prefer coffee, but remembered that the last coffee she'd had after playing was made with a particularly nasty cheap brand of instant coffee, and she'd decided to steer clear of it.

"I understand you're involved with the children's summer camp," she said, as she waited for the kettle to boil.

"I am, yes! Such fun, bringing on all the young talent. Of course we have a very gifted person doing the actual coaching. I just help with the admin and the games and prizes."

"Is that Gavin?" asked Tamsin, all wide-eyed.

"Oh no! Gavin wouldn't demean himself at the summer camp! No, it's Jonathan. You've met him, haven't you?"

"Jonathan? Ah yes - I played with him the other week." Tamsin poured the tea and sipped hers gingerly. "What do you think happened, Margaret? Who could have done this to Lesley? Who had she upset?"

Margaret tutted, "Any number of people. She really won't be much missed." She bit into a stiff wedge of gingerbread. "But if you mean who did it, well, *obviously* that had nothing to do with anyone from Tom's. She probably just tripped and fell, and some stranger came along and .. and put the ball in her mouth." She brushed the crumbs off her bosom and her lap.

"Why would anyone do that? Wouldn't anyone call for help if they found her? Wouldn't you?"

"There are some troublemakers around. Perhaps someone from the cottages along the road who resented all the comings and goings at the club. There are some teenagers there - who knows what they might do!" she tutted. "They'd probably think it a great joke, to push a tennis ball .. to push .." She was finding it hard to finish the sentence.

At this moment they heard the creak of the iron gate, and Tamsin realised her chance of finding out anything material from Margaret was gone.

The players started to arrive, and they made a sorry sight. Nobody seemed to know quite how they should behave in this weird situation, but none of them wanted to miss out on their tennis fix.

And some were clearly desperate for the latest gossip!

"Bessie, I wasn't expecting you today?" said Victoria to someone who evidently hadn't been to a session for ages.

Bessie opened her mouth to say something vacuous about 'just feeling like some tennis', thought better of it, and said instead with a throaty chuckle, "Well, I just had to come down and find out what's going on!"

This broke the ice, and soon everyone was talking at once.

Bryan protested that he was shocked beyond measure, but that really Lesley had not been the easiest person to get on with. A few people nodded.

"When's the funeral?" asked Victoria. "We ought to attend, I suppose."

Neil responded to this question by saying he had no idea. The body had not been released. "We'll have to organise something sometime - a memorial or something ..." he ended lamely.

Toto was almost overcome with emotion, and fussed round Glenda till she told him to go away. He went to the corner of the pavilion and slumped in a chair, doing a fine Noel Coward impersonation of despair, one arm dangling over the arm of the chair, and the back of his hand to his brow. Neil went over and tried to get him somewhere near reality by starting to discuss the new treasurer vacancy and the need to fill it fast.

Turning to Tamsin, who was offering round the flat slices of unin-spiring gingerbread, he said, "Er, Tamsin, isn't it. You're not good at figures by any chance, are you?"

She shook her head with a sweet smile. "Can just about work out the calories in a slice of cake, but that's my limit, I'm afraid." And she moved on quickly, in case Neil was serious.

"Amanda, are you going to actually *play* this evening," demanded Glenda, "or are you going to spend the time gossiping?"

"Oh, I'd love to play! Absolutely! May I partner you, Glenda?"

"We'll need two more people who would rather play tennis than yapper on ..." Glenda scanned the gathering, and summoned Victoria and Julia.

"No children today, Julia?" asked Victoria as they picked up their racquets.

"I really thought it would be better not," Julia said quietly. "I'm finding it hard enough myself. I don't want to be dealing with nightmares from the children too."

Margaret was being as motherly as possible, offering cups of tea and slabs of gingerbread. As the gingerbread looked like a flat brown book, and the jam in the tarts had burnt, Tamsin escaped having to eat any by snatching the tray of tarts and passing them round.

"Shocking thing," muttered Margaret as she pushed past Gavin with the gingerbread and a mug of tea, just as Tamsin was passing behind him with her tray. Gavin leant over Margaret and said, "Had your fingers in the till, my dear?" and gave a sly smile. "Is that why Lesley wanted to talk to you?"

As Tamsin carefully logged this strange remark of Gavin's, Margaret snorted, "Well, *really!*" and headed for Toto and Neil. Being used to Gavin's teasing she didn't usually take what he said too seri-ously, but she was still offended. "Neil," she declared, "You have to do something about Gavin. I really can't put up with him much longer." She folded her arms across her ample frontage and clamped her mouth shut.

Neil was all for pouring oil on the troubled waters. "My dear

Margaret! Everyone's upset today. You needn't take anything seriously - least of all, Gavin."

Toto fanned his face with his hand. "I'm definitely upset. It's *so* awful!"

Neil cast his eyes heavenwards as he got up to steer Margaret back to her table. "Why don't you have a game? Look, Tamsin is over there, and perhaps Bryan and I can join you both."

Tamsin jumped to attention, keen to make up the four, and passed Margaret her racquet bag. "Come on, Margaret, let's show 'em!" she said, as they all made their way to the clay court, glowing deep red in the flood-lights, all the space, trees, and hedges beyond lurking in the pitch black.

And for a short while, with the sounds of bat on ball and laughter from the two courts, all thoughts of murder were shelved as Tom's players immersed themselves in their first love.

CHAPTER TWENTY-THREE

By the time Tamsin, comfortably warmed up, had finished her set of tennis and started back to the pavilion, she heard Victoria and Gavin in an intense exchange in the darkness near the hedge. Bending down to tie her shoelace, she listened as carefully as she could.

"I never stole *anything!*" hissed Victoria.

"That's not what my informant told me .." Gavin provoked her.

"It was my first job. I *borrowed* some money from the tea kitty. I was *always* going to give it back!"

"But not fast enough, eh?"

"It was years ago. What's possessed you to bring it up now, Gavin?"

"Oh," he said airily, "I believe the police are connecting Lesley's death with her claim that money had been stolen." He stared right at her and with a set face, said, "That's all."

Victoria turned on her heel and ran back to the pavilion to fetch her jacket, saying as she barged past Tamsin, "I'm awfully sorry - nasty headache just come on. See you next week," and fled to the cars.

"Bye, Victoria," said Tamsin, turning to look after the fleeing figure. She decided to visit the Ladies and went along the path to the toilet block, puzzled that Victoria should take Gavin's jibe so seriously.

There was a single lamp lighting the path, and she jumped when she sensed some figures in the gloom beyond the pool of light. 'Looks like my other shoelace needs tying,' she thought, as she bent to the task. The lace was stubborn and wouldn't unknot, so she fiddled for some time, her ears on stalks.

"I think you've gone too far!" whispered the easily recognisable voice of Amanda. "You dote on Glenda, and now look what's happened."

Tamsin could hear Toto wailing quietly. "I don't know what you're talking about! I'd do anything to protect Glenda, and people are making nasty suggestions, that's all."

"But how could you *do* that to Lesley?"

"Do what?" Toto pulled back. "What can you mean?" He gasped loudly, "Are you accusing me of *murder?*" he said with a dramatic flourish.

"No, of course not," whispered Amanda. "The ball thing. That's what I mean. You must have done that."

"Whyever do you think I had anything to do with it all. Your imagination is running away with you, my dear Amanda."

"Because," Amanda hissed, "I saw your car driving away from here that night."

Toto sounded aghast. "What were *you* doing here?"

"I'd agreed to play with Glenda that night. Work on our court positions before the next tournament, you know. Only I was running late .."

"Are you saying Glenda was here ... earlier?" He pressed the back of his hand to his forehead.

"Well, I don't know. By the time I got here those teenagers from the cottages had discovered Lesley, and were all standing about with their bikes, jeering and ringing the police. I never saw Glenda. And in all the hoo-hah I forgot to ask her about it the next day ..."

"Don't mention this to anyone," said Toto abruptly, and flounced back to the pavilion just as Tamsin thought she couldn't fiddle with her shoelace a moment longer.

She straightened up. "Oh, hi Amanda, didn't see you there," she fibbed. "Was that Toto? He looked upset."

"I think that Toto has something to answer for," said Amanda through gritted teeth, and marched back to the pavilion. The marching didn't look quite as splendid as Amanda hoped, as it was more of a waddle.

By the time Tamsin had visited the Ladies and got back again, she hoped that some of the tension would have died down. She was astonished by Amanda and Toto's conversation. There seemed to be the suggestion that all three of them were at the club that evening, right at the critical time. More digging was required!

As she climbed the creaking wooden steps to the old building, she could hear the courts were in use again. Bryan and Toto were playing Neil and Gavin. There was a lot of hard hitting from the men. Perhaps they were getting rid of their feelings by knocking seven bells out of the balls.

Julia jumped up as Tamsin came in. "Make up a four with me and Margaret?" she asked. "Bessie's ready to play too." She looked around her. "Oh, where's Margaret gone? She was here a moment ago .."

Tamsin peered into the darkness beyond the grass court. "Isn't that her over there? Talking to Glenda?"

"Everything's upside down," sighed Julia. "Those two never talk to each other unless they have to."

"They certainly seem to have plenty to say to each other at the moment." Shoelace-tying was of no use now. So Tamsin resorted to studying the two women's body language from afar. Margaret was leaning forward and gesticulating, while Glenda's arms were folded tightly across her thin chest.

Julia was saying, "Just one set, Tamsin, then I'm going home. It really is miserable." She put a trembling hand to her cheek. "Everyone seems to be at each others' throats! Awful things are being said."

"What have you heard, Julia?" Tamsin asked her friend quietly. "Has anyone said anything - useful?"

"Not really. Margaret seems to be upset with everyone. And Toto looks like he's walking toward the gallows. Gavin's been going through the supplies of tennis balls - I don't know what he expected to find there,

I'm sure. If you ask me," she said under her breath, "Glenda's covering something up. Now, I'm not saying she *did* it! Just .. I don't know .. something fishy's going on."

Tamsin nodded slowly, then put a hand on Julia's back and said, "Come on, let's go and knock the covers off a few balls, like the men are doing - I'm sure we'll all feel a bit better for it!"

"Look, here's Bessie. Bessie, would you like to tell Margaret she's on?"

Bessie toddled off towards the grass court to fetch Margaret. Seeing her approach, the two women stepped apart and started to head back, Glenda looking nonchalant, while steam seemed to be coming from Margaret's ears.

And there was plenty of hard hitting when they got to the clay court and began to play. But it wasn't till their set was over and they walked back to the now almost empty pavilion, that Tamsin had a chance to talk to Margaret again. Julia and Bessie were walking ahead of them, and she leant over and spoke quietly.

"I gather there were a few of the members here that night - the night Lesley died." She decided to toss in the remark and wait for a result. As her father used to say, 'Run it up the flagpole and see who salutes it!'

And she scored an immediate hit.

Margaret stopped dead in her tracks and turned, wide-eyed, to Tamsin. "Who said that?" she demanded.

"Um, I can't remember who it was. Just general chitchat in the pavilion, I think," she prevaricated, frowning as if trying to remember.

"I've no doubt the police will be *very* interested to hear that," Margaret snapped. "But I expect they already know. I believe they've already been questioning Neil and Gavin." She sighed loudly.

"But Neil was away skiing, wasn't he?"

"Oh no! He got back on the Friday, just before .. erm .. Before."

"Really?" Tamsin chewed her lip thoughtfully, as Margaret went on, "I suppose they'll be wanting to talk to all of us, before long."

"I suppose you're right," said Tamsin, sadly zipping her hot pink racquet into its hot pink bag, wondering why murder seemed to follow her around. "I'd so hoped to join and just enjoy playing tennis."

"Didn't we all!" said Margaret fervently.

"Ah well, thank you for the game, Margaret. I'm going home to my dogs and some supper. Night Bessie, nice to meet you. Julia, love to Romeo and the kids! See you next week?"

"Indeedy! And I hope that Sara will be back from College by then and she can come."

"That'll be lovely! Then perhaps we'll be seeing Andrew again, too!" Tamsin gave a cheeky grin, swung her racquet bag over her shoulder and set off for the *Top Dogs* van. Getting in, she leant back in her seat with a sigh, before turning the key and sliding off into the darkness along the narrow back roads of Herefordshire.

CHAPTER TWENTY-FOUR

Tamsin and Emerald had both been busy with home visits on Thursday, Tamsin taking the dogs with her in the *Top Dogs* van so she could give them a run on the Common on the way home, and Emerald, wrapped up in coat, gloves, and helmet, riding Tamsin's old sit-up-and-beg bike, her yoga mat rolled up in the bike basket.

So the leek and potato soup that Tamsin had made earlier in the day was most welcome when they arrived home that evening. It was good to be back indoors, out of the cold March weather, warm and dry. By mutual consent, the subjects of tennis, Tom's, and murders were all taboo while they enjoyed their soup, along with some of the sourdough bread they'd bought from *Hilda's Homebakes* last Saturday, now toasted. All was quiet as they sipped and crunched.

Until, that is, the dogs burst into song as they heard a car pull up outside their little house in Pippin Lane. Emerald reached a languid arm out and twitched the curtain.

"It's Feargal!" she exclaimed, and jumped up from the sofa, dislodging the previously purring Opal as she unwound her feet from under her.

Tamsin said *"Thank you!"* to stop the dogs barking and smiled to herself. "I guess it's a good thing I made a bucket of soup! We've still got plenty of that nice bread of Hilda's anyway." And she got up to dish up another helping of the food for their guest.

"Your radar is working well," she grinned at Feargal, as he arrived through the door and was being helped out of his coat by Emerald.

"Oh, am I interrupting your dinner?" he asked innocently, with a twinkle in his eye and a crooked grin. He gave an exaggerated shiver, "Brass monkey weather out there!"

"Come on, let's go into the warm. The fire's on in the living room." And she loaded Feargal's dinner onto a tray to carry in.

He settled himself down on the sofa, giving the dogs a friendly pat each, and said, "You can tell me what went down last night while I plough through this lot. It smells delicious!" And without more ado he started eating.

"The atmosphere was very fraught, I have to say. But there were quite a few bitchy remarks about our esteemed Treasurer. They seemed to feel safe in expressing their views, now she's not around any more. Nobody seemed to like her much."

"Clearly someone didn't like her at all!" added Emerald, as she arranged Opal on her lap again.

"I was quite surprised at who confessed to disliking her. Gavin, Margaret. We know Glenda didn't like her. But then Glenda doesn't seem to like anyone."

"Sounds promising," Feargal mumbled through a mouthful of hot potato.

"The thing is - I overheard a couple of interesting conversations."

Emerald stopped stroking Opal for a moment till the cat nudged her hand with her tiny moist pink nose and she resumed.

"First of all Gavin was .. threatening Victoria. Not sure why. But it seems she'd got the sack from her first job for dipping into the tea money. Long time ago. Victoria claimed she'd only borrowed it. She was terribly upset and flounced out."

"Curious," said Feargal, tucking into another doorstep of toast.

"And Gavin also made a sly remark to Margaret, which infuriated her."

A raised eyebrow from Feargal had her continue, "Gavin suggested that Lesley had asked to see Margaret, and that perhaps she'd had her hands in the till."

Feargal swallowed, "This Gavin sounds a stirrer. Not quite the suave gentleman he put across to us when we visited him."

"Then - much worse. Amanda was telling off Toto, accusing him of doing the trick with the ball. It seems that both of them were there that evening!"

"No!" said Emerald, with round eyes to match her round mouth.

"Apparently Glenda and Amanda had arranged to meet to practice. Amanda was late and when she got there the village lads had discovered the body. Toto was driving away as she arrived."

"Wow!"

"So Amanda accused him of doing the ball thing. He was hopping. Suddenly lost his camp manner and became positively menacing, telling her to keep this to herself. With a kind of 'or else' tagged on."

"And what about Glenda?" asked Emerald.

"Nobody knows if she was there or not. Amanda forgot to ask her in all the fuss, and is probably too scared to now. She was suggesting that Toto did the thing with the ball, but not the murder. Though why should he?"

Emerald shook her head slowly. "No idea. The tennis ball really points to someone from Tom's being involved. Why would he do that?"

"Doesn't make sense," agreed Feargal, who was now leaning back in his seat, hands clasped across his full tummy.

"But it's very odd that two - maybe all three - of them were there."

"Right at the crucial moment!"

"And why did no-one know this?"

"Presumably they're all keeping quiet about it. I guess Inspector Hawkins probably knows. They must have been interviewing them all?"

"But," Tamsin leant forward over Moonbeam on her lap, "maybe no-one has spilt the beans! I only know because I overheard Amanda ranting."

"A little bird told me .." Feargal began, but was interrupted by Tamsin and Emerald simultaneously.

"You mean a little mole!" they giggled.

"Ok, a little black furry thing," he laughed. "Well, it seems that they're closing in on Glenda. So perhaps they have evidence that she was there."

"Oh, but Glenda didn't do it. I'm sure of that." Tamsin said firmly, as she sat back in her chair again.

"How do you know?" asked Emerald.

"I'm just sure she didn't. Didn't need to. She could wither anyone with the way she talks to them. She murders their souls," she said dramatically, "and leaves their bodies behind."

Emerald shuddered. "She really sounds most unpleasant."

"I can vouch for that, having met her," agreed Feargal. "But that's an interesting theory - that you can be so nasty that you can murder people with a glare and shut them up that way."

"Don't you agree?" asked Tamsin.

"I think you could be right. I think she's so supremely arrogant that she wouldn't need to stoop to killing anyone."

"Anyway, she's not on the committee and doesn't have access to the club's money," Emerald pointed out.

"That's true," agreed Tamsin. "But we're only *guessing* that the money had anything to do with it. Maybe it was something else entirely."

Feargal stroked Banjo's head as it had come to rest on his knee. Tamsin felt a warm fuzzy feeling rise up in her at the sight of her shy collie responding so well to their friend.

"You know," he said, "they seem to think that the murder was manslaughter anyway. That it was a physical fight that ended unfortunately. No-one could have deliberately pushed her onto that cut branch."

"But whoever it was must have been very angry," said Emerald. "I mean, that must have been quite a forceful shove?"

Feargal hemmed and hawed. "Unless Lesley tripped and lost her balance. However murderous you felt, you couldn't rely on that push doing for her! And we're back to wondering whether it was one person, or two people together .."

"Or two people separately," sighed Tamsin. "I think we need to sleep on this new information. Maybe we'll get a shaft of light in the morning!"

And the friends spent the rest of the evening chatting about more innocuous things, like discussing Tamsin's next dog training article for the *Malvern Mercury*. They ended up wrapped in duvets and nursing mugs of hot chocolate, watching an old black and white film - one of the great Ealing comedies from the heyday of British film-making, marvelling at the innocence of films 'back in the day' and rocking in their chairs with laughter.

CHAPTER TWENTY-FIVE

No flash of blinding light or revelation came to Tamsin in the night. She busied herself with a home visit in the morning, to a Basset Hound called Frodo who didn't seem to want to get out of his bed. She reckoned he had trouble with his elongated back and recommended a Vet check and a Canine Massage Therapist to help, along with some fun he could have with his owner without stressing his back.

Then she had her favourite class of the week - her Malvern Puppy Class - which fed her soul! She'd brought Quiz with her, who lay peacefully on her mat, next to an open pot of treats. Quiz loved puppies, and Tamsin was able to demonstrate - without saying anything at all - how the new puppy owners could expect their dog to behave.

This was followed by a return visit to a lady with a designer dog who didn't like being left alone, out on the Hereford road. So it wasn't until early evening, when the sun had already set, and she was leaving the expensive dog whose issues were just as real as the cheapest mongrel's - despite the owner's idea that she had paid extra for a perfect dog - that she found herself heading towards Tom's.

"I just want to take another look at that hedge," she explained to Quiz, who was riding behind her in the back of the van.

She parked in front of Tom's, and took Quiz for a search along the hedgerow. "The police will have covered it, but you never know," she told her dog as she pointed her to the hedge and said "Find!"

As Quiz was busily snuffling around the base of the hedge, just over the ditch, a young boy on a bike pulled up.

"Wotcher doin' Miss?" he asked, his voice distorted by the lollipop whose stick was poking out of the side of his mouth.

Tamsin knew well the value of the observational skills of small boys, and turned to him with a smile.

"I'm just looking for something someone may have dropped here - last week," she added meaningfully.

"Is that a police dog? Is 'e wicked?" the boy hesitated, holding on firmly to his handlebars.

"No," Tamsin laughed. "She's just a really good search dog."

The boy gave a quiet "Coo!" and watched silently as Quiz lifted her head and air-scented round the fork of a tree growing out of the hedge.

The lad dropped his bike on the grass and pointed to where Quiz was sniffing. "Yer mean this?"

Tamsin stepped forward and could just see a piece of paper, tucked under the bark.

"Me bruvver fahnd it near where that old bat was *murdered*. 'E put it there. Is it a clue? Will there be a reward?"

Thanking Quiz, Tamsin stepped forward and retrieved the piece of paper, removing it carefully - after a week outside it was damp and soft. The boy leaned over her hands to see what his brother had hidden. Easing it open carefully Tamsin saw with surprise that it was a bookie's receipt for a largish sum of money - several hundred pounds. And it had Margaret's name on it. Margaret! She whipped out a new plastic poo bag, "How useful you dogs are!" she muttered to Quiz, and slid the paper carefully inside, before folding the black bag and pushing it deep in her security pocket inside her waistband.

"Thanks kiddo!" she said, and fished a pound coin out of her pocket, tossing it to the small boy. In one motion he caught it, trousered it, leapt on his bike and skedaddled.

Her smile turned to a frown as she started to walk back towards her van. So Margaret had a gambling problem, with all the money troubles that naturally stemmed from it. She remembered her father telling her that as a teenager he had been playing golf with a bookie, and thinking it was the grown-up thing to do, suggested, "Five bob on this round?" - a lot of money for a youngster back then. The bookie was a kindly man. "See that Bentley over there in the car park, son? How do you think I can afford that? Don't bet!" And her father never did again.

She clipped one end of the lead onto Quiz as she walked, the other end being attached to her belt. There was another car parked next to the *Top Dogs* van now. 'I didn't know they played tonight?' she thought idly. As she reached her van a dark figure slid out from behind it, saying in a menacing voice, "You've found something! You'd better give it to me."

Before she realised what was happening, Tamsin was pushed down onto the ground, and found the full weight of Margaret sitting on top of her. She grabbed Tamsin's hands and wrenched them behind her back before tying them with some twine she'd pulled out of her pocket.

"I haven't got anything," Tamsin protested, desperately trying to free her hands, kicking out with her legs. It had little effect - Margaret was a large lady. Quiz barked and jumped about, but she would never dream of biting a person, so the most she did was muzzle-punch Margaret's arm a couple of times.

"What on earth are you doing, Margaret?" protested Tamsin, still struggling, becoming aware of the alcohol on Margaret's heavy breaths.

"I've been finding more out about you, our sweet new member!" Margaret shifted her bulk to squash Tamsin's legs and stop them moving then started to feel in her pockets. "You aren't what you seem. I talked to Julia. Oh, she was all too ready to sing your praises - *as a detective!*" she growled.

"I'm not a detective - I'm just a dog trainer. Ouch!" said Tamsin, wincing as her legs were pressed into the tarmac. "You've got it all wrong."

"I don't think so," hissed Margaret. "Get up," she ordered, pulling Tamsin up by her coat. She plunged her hand into another pocket, said

"Ooer! What in ...?" and pulled out a handful of clammy cubes of cheese which had got squashed while Tamsin was being sat on.

"I told you. I'm a dog trainer," Tamsin repeated, as Margaret shoved her along roughly in front of her, up the path to the tennis club. The place was in total darkness. Quiz trotted after Tamsin, attached to her belt as she was. Margaret didn't notice the collie till they got to the old store shed, then saying, "Stupid dog!" she fastened Tamsin to a heavy net post, shut them both in and turned to go.

"I'll leave you to reconsider. You'll get hungry soon enough. Perhaps you'll have to eat your dog, hahaha!" she cackled and stepped out, shutting the door and leaving Tamsin and Quiz in the pitch black.

Tamsin listened to her footsteps going back down the path, then she heard the slam of a car door and an engine starting up. Margaret drove away into the night. It was all quiet.

Tamsin let out a deep sigh. Recalling the black and white films they'd been watching in Pippin Lane, she said, "'Well, here's another nice mess you've gotten me into'!" to Quiz, who sat beside her. As her eyes adjusted to the dark, Tamsin could make out Quiz's one erect ear, and her heart swelled as she knew she was not alone. She thought of all the scrapes Laurel and Hardy had found themselves in and escaped from, and it cheered her.

"Now then, Quizzy, what are we going to do? Margaret has clearly gone off her trolley. So we need to be outa here before she gets back. I wonder where she's gone?" She shook her head, "But that doesn't matter now. Let me think ... I've got my phone, but it's zipped into my trouser pocket. Can't get that out till my hands are free. Free hands ... hmm!" Tamsin suddenly realised the answer. "This is your moment, Quiz!" She swivelled a little on the cold floor of the shed. "Get behind!" she said, and Quiz obediently got as far behind her as she could, in all the mess of tennis nets, posts, gardening tools and boxes of balls.

Tamsin wiggled her fingers to attract Quiz to her hands. "Quiz! Cut!" she said, straining to hold her hands as far apart as she could, exposing the twine tied round them and which was now cutting into her wrists.

Tamsin felt Quiz push her warm soft muzzle into the space between her hands, her fingers feeling the collie's sharp whiskers, and the tensing of the jaw muscles as Quiz latched on to the twine and started to bite.

"Ouch! Mind me!" she said as a tooth caught her hand in the narrow space. Quiz jumped back, worried she'd hurt her beloved Tamsin.

"It's ok, Quizzy, you're fine - cut! Cut!" Tamsin clenched her teeth to make sure she didn't cry out again. The twine was biting into her wrists as she pulled and the dog worked at it, inevitably scraping Tamsin's hands again in the tight space. Her arms were aching. She bit her lip and screwed up her eyes .. then - bliss! - the twine stopped hurting. She pulled her hands apart, and the first thing she did was to wrap her arms round her rescuer and bury her face in her white mane.

"Oh, you glorious dog!" she said, giving her another big hug. "Let's get out of here now!" She scrambled to her feet and found, to her surprise, that the door was unbolted. Opening it a crack, she peeped out and listened intently.

"All clear!" she whispered, and they emerged from the shed and kept to the edge of the path before skirting behind the pavilion, seeing her van by the roadside, gleaming in the gloom.

"Ouch!" she said again, as she realised her ankle was sprained. That's what happens when a madwoman sits on you, she thought, and reaching to Quiz for support she noticed the blood dripping fast from her hand. "How will I be able to drive?" she said urgently to Quiz, as they lurked in the dark behind the pavilion. "We're going to need help, old girl," and she pulled her phone out of her pocket, seeing with relief that it hadn't suffered any damage in the tussle, and wondered who she should turn to. "Has to be someone nearby, and who won't mind dropping everything to come and help me." She looked down at Quiz, thought for a moment, and texted Jonathan.

CHAPTER TWENTY-SIX

It was only a few minutes later she got a text back.

Coming

it said. And Tamsin felt a great surge of relief through her aching body. She held Quiz close to pinch some of her body heat as she leant against the back of the pavilion and waited, shivering from the cold night air and the chill of the damp ground she was sitting on. She was pressing her coat sleeve firmly to the cut in her hand to try to stop it bleeding, and stretched her injured ankle out in front of her.

And eventually, in the still of the cold dark night, she heard a motor. It was getting louder ... a motor bike? Yes! It must be coming here!

She'd never felt happier to see a motor bike than when Manic's bike pulled up next to her van, its throaty roar dying down as it stopped, its headlights lighting the path in front of her.

Two helmeted figures jumped off the bike and the taller one who'd been riding pillion ran ahead, leading the way for his shorter friend.

"Tam-SIN?" Jonathan yelled. "TAM-sin! Where are you?"

With her good hand Tamsin unclipped the lead, and Quiz ran forward to greet her friend Jonathan, and bring him round the pavilion.

"Am I glad to see you!" she beamed at him. "Hi Manic," she added, as Manic joined them.

"What on earth's happened? Are you hurt?" Jonathan demanded.

"A bit. Margaret went mad and attacked me then tied me up." She held up her bitten hand, the red weals showing on the wrists.

"Let me look at your hands .."

"Ouch! I'm afraid Quiz's teeth caught a bit of skin, but it's ok. And my ankle got a bit squashed. I'm just not sure how I can drive."

"We need to get that cut looked at," Jonathan began, turning her hand to peer at the damage. "Why did Quiz bite you?"

"She didn't! Quiz would never bite me!" protested Tamsin. "But there's no time to explain now - the mad one's coming back. We have to get away!"

"Give me your keys! I can drive your van."

Tamsin felt in her coat pocket with her good hand. "No keys! She went through my pockets. Must have chucked them out .."

"We'll never find them in the dark - and you say we have to move fast," said Manic, ever practical.

Jonathan ran his fingers through his hair in exasperation. "What can we do?"

"It's all ok," said Manic, calm as ever. "Tamsin and her dog can go in the sidecar."

"You've got a sidecar?" asked Tamsin with surprise. "Will it be safe for Quiz?"

"Sure! I use it for transporting hedgehogs," he beamed. "Nice to have something less prickly in there this evening ... and it's pretty safe. There's a seat belt, and you can hang on tight to Quiz. I won't drive fast."

In the distance they could hear a car. "We need to move. Now!" said Tamsin urgently, and Jonathan scooped her up and ran to the bike carrying her. He lowered her into the sidecar. Quiz hopped in and sat between her legs as Manic started the bike. Jonathan leapt on the back and they'd moved off into the night before the incoming car arrived.

It was only a few minutes before they were back in Jonathan's yard.

He helped Tamsin and Quiz out of the sidecar and she leant heavily on him as they went to the kitchen.

"I think that will be the first and last time I travel in a sidecar," said Tamsin. "I'm frozen!"

"Here, let's get you warm," and Jonathan moved a big old rocking chair next to the Aga and helped Tamsin into it. He found a stool to rest her leg on. "Hot drink!" he said firmly, and starting making coffee.

"I'll do that," said Manic. "You dress her wound."

Teal had ventured out from his bed beside the Aga as they'd all come in, and was hesitantly inspecting Quiz. As she was a bitch, and such a laid-back one at that, this made the meeting easier, and it wasn't long before both dogs were lying against the cooker contentedly.

"It was lucky you were here," said Tamsin as Jonathan gently bathed her cut and decided what size plaster to put over it.

"It was *very* lucky that Manic was here," corrected Jonathan. "My car conked out this afternoon and he came over to fix it. Otherwise I'd only have had my little Ferguson."

"And that would have been an even colder and bumpier ride than the sidecar!" Manic assured her, as Tamsin gratefully accepted a steaming mug of coffee from him with her good hand.

Jonathan straightened up from wrapping a long horse bandage round and round Tamsin's ankle and foot. "That should help keep it stable. Now. What is going on?" He leant back in the chair he'd drawn up beside her. "You have to explain it to us."

So Tamsin described the events of the evening, what she had found in the hedge, how Margaret was seriously implicated in Lesley's murder, and how the woman had completely flipped and imprisoned her. And she gazed softly at her sleeping dog, telling her amazed listeners exactly how she had freed her.

"So you told her to cut the string - and she did?" Manic said with astonishment.

"I see now how you got bitten," said Jonathan, and seeing Tamsin's scowl, instantly amended it. "I mean, how the teeth caught your hand."

Tamsin smiled beatifically at him. "Good thing it bled so much, it cleaned itself. I was bitten by a cat once, and it didn't bleed. Few days later my hand was like a boxing glove!"

"I think it's time we went and had a word with this Margaret," said Jonathan firmly. "I know where she lives. I've been there to discuss the kids' camp."

"No! We can't! She's a nutcase!" Tamsin was surprised to feel such fear.

"She can't capture all of us." Manic folded his arms, exposing the tattoos on his wiry but muscular forearms. "Let's go and find out what she's at. We're more likely right now to get the story out of her. She's probably panicking if she arrived back to find your van and no you."

"And we're less threatening than the police may seem," Jonathan nodded.

"I suppose you're right."

"You're not frightened, are you? Tamsin Kernick, intrepid investigator?" he teased gently.

"It wasn't nice. But I feel safe now. And a lot warmer, thank you!" She smiled up at his concerned face. "But you know what? I think I should call Feargal - my reporter friend, remember?"

Jonathan nodded, and Tamsin went on, "He should be there too. I can do that now before we set off."

CHAPTER TWENTY-SEVEN

Jonathan chose a warm duvet jacket from the porch for Tamsin to wear for the journey. "Don't want you freezing again," he smiled as he helped her bandaged hand through the sleeve, then standing right in front of her, he pulled up the jacket's zip and wedged a woolly hat down over her ears. Tamsin was touched by his warm attentiveness. She felt a tear coming, and started to see him through new eyes.

They all clambered into and onto Manic's big bike, and with a roar of the engine, they set off again into the night, Quiz neatly tucked under Tamsin's legs in the sidecar. The collie was getting used to this noisy mode of transport!

Feargal had got there in double-quick time, and was parked at the end of Margaret's road. Following Tamsin's pointing finger, Manic quietly purred his bike into the space behind him and cut the engine. Feargal jumped out of his car to greet them and get some more details beyond the sketchy outline Tamsin had given him on the phone.

Seeing her bandaged hand, he said, "You're injured, old girl!"

"I am not, yet, an old girl," she grumped. "And my dog savagely attacked me," she grinned.

"Now that I can't believe," Feargal reached out to fondle Quiz's head, while Tamsin briefly filled him in on the main details, including the book-ie's receipt, her capture, and her wonderful dog who rescued her.

Feargal was concerned, but suitably impressed. "Good for you, Quiz!"

"I can see the light's on in her house," said Jonathan, peering down the quiet street.

"I don't want to bring Quiz in .." Tamsin began, feeling fiercely defensive of her precious dog.

"Let's hop her into my car," said Feargal. "She'll be ok there, won't she?"

"Be sure to lock it!" fussed Tamsin as she shut the car door on her puzzled dog. She bent to stare through the window, "Mind the car, Quizzy! We'll be back in a minute."

Having also stowed the two crash helmets in the car, Feargal held his key in the air to demonstrate as he clicked the button and the car lights flashed. "Poor you. This has upset you. Not surprising!" He put a hand on her shoulder.

She smiled gratefully at her friend, and this time it was Feargal she lent on to limp down the road to Margaret's house.

When Margaret opened the door, her face was a picture. First she saw Jonathan, and recognised him. But he wasn't smiling as usual. Then she saw Manic beside him in his motorbike leathers. Whoever he was, he definitely wasn't smiling, and he looked quite frightening. Then behind them she saw Feargal supporting Tamsin, and saying "Oh God!" she tried to slam the door.

But Manic was too quick for her and had his tough motorbike boot already wedged in the door. Margaret sagged and backed up as they all filed in. They went into her living room and Tamsin hobbled to a chair.

"You can't wriggle out of this, you know, Margaret. You attacked me and imprisoned me. Whatever else you've done, that's enough to get you locked up."

Margaret reached for the glass of brandy she'd been drinking before they came, and took a hearty glug.

"You wouldn't understand .." she began.

"Try us." Feargal responded through clenched teeth.

Margaret took a deep breath, stared at the fire, and it all rushed out. "I owed some money. You don't need to know why. Just that I did. And they wanted it back. So I borrowed some from the club to tide me over. I had to! It was just for a short while. I was going to pay it back! I had to pay the debt, you see. Had to." She sighed. "But Snootypants Lesley found out from her flipping spreadsheets. She summoned me to the club and demanded an explanation. We were standing by the cars. She said she'd denounce me to everyone. She wanted to hound me out of the club! Me!" Margaret sniffed loudly and took another swig of her drink. "She's never appreciated me - all the work I put in. Saw her chance. She jabbed me on the shoulder with her thin pointy finger." Margaret pulled an ugly face and jabbed her own chubby finger as if prodding someone. "I wasn't putting up with *that!* I mean to say ... So I pushed her away from me. Silly woman tripped and fell backwards." She spread out her hands as if it had nothing to do with her. "It was dark. She fell back into a ditch. I certainly wasn't going to stoop to helping her out again. So I went. That's it."

She smiled and settled back in her chair, with a smug expression.

"But that's not it, Margaret," said Jonathan.

"Lesley *died!*" said Feargal.

"And it was you who caused it," Tamsin was surprised to find how cold her voice was.

"I wasn't to know!" Margaret retorted in a shrill voice. "How was I to know? It was her own fault. She prodded me. She .. she .."

"She was doing her job." Jonathan couldn't keep the look of disgust from his face.

"You'd stolen money," added Manic, speaking for the first time. "Sounds as if she was looking for an explanation."

"Maybe she was going to give you time to repay the money!" said Tamsin. "Maybe, if you'd given her a chance, she'd have helped you."

"Ooh, not her. She was only interested in herself." Margaret took another large gulp of brandy and set her shoulders back. "You don't know the half of it - how she's put me down over the years. Inge-ratitude, I call it. There! In-grathitood." Her words were beginning to slur as she found herself drifting ever further from reality.

Jonathan stepped forward and removed the glass from her. "I think you've had enough of that, Margaret. You're going to need your wits about you when the police interview you."

"Police?" Margaret looked startled. "Why police?"

"You killed a woman. Or at least fatally injured her. Then you callously stuck a tennis ball in her mouth and left her there to die."

"What? No! No no, I never did that tennis ball thing. That's awful. Not me. I'm not like that. *Oh* no!" she gave a firm shake of the head, reached for the glass of brandy and found it not there. She looked puzzled.

"So who did?" asked Feargal.

"I have nooo idea. As far as I was aware, Lesley was just fine." Margaret frowned, and added. "She didn't say much after she fell in the ditch."

"Didn't say much, or didn't say anything?" enquired Manic quietly.

"Oh, I don't know! Now you're trying to confuse me. Who are you, anyway? You shouldn't be here." She glowered at Manic and flicked her finger at him in dismissal.

"It's time to end this charade," said Feargal. "You've said enough. Let's get you down to the station. You're ready to hand yourself in, I take it?"

"What for? I haven't done anything," Margaret bleated, folded her arms and stamped her feet.

"In that case," said Feargal, slipping his phone out of his pocket and dialling, "the police can come to you." He turned away as he spoke to the police station. He was quickly put through to the duty Sergeant who knew him well, and listened to his story with interest, especially that there'd been a confession.

"They'll be here presently. But there's something else we need to know: what have you done with Tamsin's keys?"

"Why do you think I have Tamsin's keys? What would I want with Tamsin's keys?" said Margaret huffily.

"You were going through my pockets, do you remember?"

"Oh, I was looking to see if you'd found anything in the hedge. That's all. I didn't actually *take* anything. I'm not a thief! I'm a fine upsitting, er upshtanding, shitishen." She nodded vigorously, then put a hand to her head to keep it still.

Feargal turned to Tamsin. "We'll go back to Tom's and search, now we have time. I've got a torch in the car."

"And it'll be a chance for Quiz to shine again," smiled Tamsin.

"Anyhow!" barked Margaret. "How did you get out? I'm good at tying knots - learned that in the Girl Guides." She said expansively, then turned and looked slightly cross-eyed at Tamsin, and frowned.

"My dog was with me. And as I told you, I'm a dog trainer, remember?"

"Your stupid dog untied my knots?" Margaret appeared insulted.

"Better than that. She just cut the cords. And she's far from stupid."

"Stupid dog!" Margaret huffed. At which everyone fell into silence, awaiting the bee-baw of the police car, which made it from Malvern in record time and halted outside the door, leaving its blue lights flashing for all the neighbours to see, as they twitched their curtains and wondered what had happened to the old dear at no. 17.

In came the large sergeant, his yellow waistcoat bristling with walkie-talkies, tasers, pepper spray, and handcuffs, which last he now applied to Margaret's chubby wrists as he cautioned her. She became strangely acquiescent, giving a sly, drunken, smile to her captor.

And as he led her out to his car, he turned and winked at Tamsin and Feargal, saying very quietly, "Hawkins will bless you!"

They all spilled out into the road and the sergeant secured the house and pocketed the keys. As they watched the yellow and blue checked car drive off, still flashing blue, they became aware of the curtains closing again along the street.

"Wonder whether he was joking, about Hawkins?" mused Feargal with a smile, as they started walking up the road, Jonathan standing in as Tamsin's crutch on this occasion.

"And I wonder if she was telling the truth about the tennis ball," said Jonathan, still shocked by the revelations.

"She actually could be," said Tamsin slowly. "You see, I happen to know that there were two - possibly three - other people there that evening. Presumably after Margaret had left."

They all turned and stared at her. "Who?" they choroused.

"Toto, Amanda and possibly Glenda."

"How do you know?" demanded Feargal.

"Know what?" said Jonathan. "I think Tamsin's had enough for this evening. We need to get her home. All that can wait. Your Inspector friend will obviously want to talk to her about it all - plenty of time to tell him. It's such a nasty thing to do, but I don't know if defiling a dead body is something they'll pursue."

"I know about that," chipped in Feargal. "It's not actually against the law. There's a list of things that *can* be prosecuted, but shoving a ball in a corpse's mouth is not one of them, as I recall. So probably they won't bother."

Tamsin shivered, and leant heavily against Jonathan.

"Come on!" said Feargal. "Let's go and find these keys. Can you drive her home when we've found them, Jonathan? I'll have copy to file!" he laughed.

"You can travel to Tom's in style in Feargal's car," smiled Manic.

It took Quiz no time to find the keys once Tamsin had led them all to the spot where she'd been attacked. Feargal set off to write his report. And Jonathan got Tamsin and her dog safely ensconced in the *Top Dogs* van to set off to Pippin Lane, with Manic following so he could bring Jonathan home again after.

"What a day!" said Tamsin, as her head lolled back onto the head-rest and she fell instantly asleep.

CHAPTER TWENTY-EIGHT

The Cake Stop was fairly full a week later when all the comfiest chairs were occupied by Tamsin and her friends arranged round a couple of tables by the big window, and the group's chatter was happy and animated.

"Charity! Bring Muffin over here - she can share Moonbeam's mat." And the three mats in the window, already bearing three dogs, soon bore Muffin as well. The four dogs happily munched their dried fish chews in companionable silence.

Jean-Philippe hovered and took their orders.

"We're getting special service today!" said Emerald, asking for her coffee.

"Don't want all of you cluttering up the counter," grinned the barista, "especially with those crutches - you are positively dangerous, Tamsin, a walking trip hazard! Now, *Madame* Charity, what will you have? A pot for one?"

"That would be perfect, my dear, thank you," beamed Charity, tucking her handbag beside her on her armchair. The smallest person had the most capacious chair, it seemed.

"Ah *Bonjour, Mademoiselle* Sara! You are home from College? Is your horse having a holiday too?"

Sara laughed. "Yes, Crystal's home too. We're borrowing one of Daddy's hunters and going for a ride tomorrow," she beamed as she turned to the tall red-headed young man beside her.

"It seems protection is needed for you young ladies," smiled Andrew with a wink.

"Not any longer, I hope!" said Tamsin. "Now the Tennis Club Tear-away is safely under lock and key."

"Your hand better?" enquired Sara. "You seem to have just a small bandage now."

"Miles better thanks. The hospital wanted to report it, but I insisted it was self-inflicted. Anyway, they gave me antibiotics to be on the safe side - as it was an injury involving a dog's teeth."

"That's her way of saying it wasn't a dog bite!" grinned Emerald.

"Well, it wasn't!" Tamsin pouted. "And what a suggestion, that my lovely Quiz should carry anything untoward in her saliva ... Anyway, it's much better, thank you. I expect all the bleeding cleaned it. The ankle will take longer though. No running for now, so no tennis. And I have to be sure to wear these supportive boots whenever I'm out." She stretched out a leg to demonstrate her rather splendid walking boots, laced up round her ankles. In so doing she dislodged one of her crutches from the arm of her chair and it clattered to the floor. Jonathan bent to pick it up for her.

Jean-Philippe simply raised a bushy black eyebrow and nodded sagely at the noise, saying *"Précisément ..."* then winked and continued taking orders. When it came to Feargal, Andrew, Jonathan, and Manic, there were mountains of food to be added to the page. Tamsin, on the other hand, was happy just to indulge herself with cake, and asked what was on offer today.

"Ah well," Jean-Philippe began. "Word has got round about what you did." Tamsin blushed modestly. "And the Three Furies have sent down one of their specials, to mark your bravery .." Tamsin was about to protest, but he added quickly, ".. *la courageuse Mademoiselle* Quiz!" and bowed to the puzzled dog, who looked up, smiled, then continued with her chew.

Everyone burst into applause and laughter, as Kylie appeared bearing a large cake. As she lowered it carefully to the table, they all stared at it in wonder. Sitting amid a jumble of tennis paraphernalia and garden tools was a very creditable coloured marzipan likeness of Quiz, with cords dangling from her mouth.

"Oh, I love it!" exclaimed Tamsin. "Here, let me get a photo before we cut it." And she whipped out her phone and started snapping, leaning this way and that to get a good angle.

"Look how they've frayed the ends of the cords!" said Emerald.

"How did they make her so realistic?" said Jonathan, in awe.

"They asked me for a photo of her, so they could get her markings right," smiled Emerald.

"You sneaky thing! And haven't they, just!" Tamsin was as delighted as a seven-year-old on her birthday. "They've got her standing-up ear exactly right, and the shape of her blaze." She tilted her head and admired the cake, then turned to gaze lovingly at the real thing, on the mat beside her chair.

Charity leaned forward. "I do believe that's fondant they've used to make the string."

"We must visit Penelope, Electra, and Damaris to thank them," Tamsin said quietly to Emerald, who nodded enthusiastically: "They're so clever!" she agreed.

"And crafty! Fancy getting a photo from you - and you never said a word!" giggled Tamsin.

And while Kylie went back to fetch a tray of plates and forks and a big knife, Jean-Philippe snapped his order book shut and bowing slightly, said, *"Deux minutes!"*

Once everyone had their drinks, and the lads were tucking into their food ('Where do they put it all?' sighed Tamsin to herself), and the cake had been sliced and dished out, Charity said into the contented silence, "Now, I think you'll have to explain it all to us, Tamsin, my dear."

Tamsin put down her mug of delicious coffee. "You've read Feargal's article in the *Mercury*, haven't you?"

"There was only so much I could say," said Feargal. "There are libel laws, you know!"

"And *sub judice*, I imagine?" asked Manic.

"That too. We have to be careful what we say when we're reporting an ongoing case."

"Ok," Tamsin said, and they all turned to look at her. "Well, I can tell you that Margaret was an unlikely gambler. She'd run up some debts and was being threatened as only bookies can threaten. So she *borrowed* the money from the Tom's account. She says she intended to pay it back, but I've no idea what with."

"Probably thought she could win it on the horses," Jonathan shook his head sadly.

"But Lesley found out. And she was a stickler for her precious figures. She'd been keeping the club's finances in order for years. She confronted Margaret over a receipt she'd found under the table in the pavilion, proving that Margaret had used the exact amount of missing money to pay her gambling debts. They argued outside the club that night. I'm sure Lesley was goaded by Margaret, and she poked her with her finger. That was too much for the rather larger Margaret, who shoved her back. That's when she fell into the ditch and struck her head on the cut branch."

Emerald shuddered and Feargal touched her hand for a moment.

"And then I do believe she turned on her heel and flounced off. She forgot to rescue the incriminating receipt from where it had fallen in the hedge. She says she didn't know Lesley was dead. And in the dark she may not have done. She certainly didn't check, or attempt to help her. She must have been overcome with fury instead of remorse, and drove off. It was only very much later that she thought the evidence Lesley had mentioned may have been somewhere there. That's when she came back and found me."

Feargal took up the tale. "She'd already been on the bottle. So she was quite irrational."

"Yes. She didn't search me properly. She was just angry!"

"What a good thing she doesn't rate dogs!" said Manic, who'd finished his toastie and was eying his slice of the splendid cake. "She never realised Quiz could help you."

"It *is* a good thing, yes!" Tamsin turned and smiled on Quiz, who was now dozing in the shafts of thin winter sunshine coming through the big plate glass window, her chin resting on Banjo's back.

"I still can't believe that you taught Quiz how to cut things!" Sara clapped her hands together.

"She taught herself really. I just labelled what she was doing so that I could use it when I wanted, and she wouldn't cut things I wanted to keep intact."

"So what's the position with Margaret," Charity was all compassion.

"She's inside, awaiting trial. Manslaughter, diminished responsibility, I believe. Not to mention drunk driving," said Feargal. "They won't be letting her out any time soon, you can be sure of that. Especially as she showed violence to Tamsin as well, causing ABH."

Emerald tilted her head enquiringly.

"Actual Bodily Harm." Feargal explained to her. "And the sentence for kidnapping alone is usually about five years."

"And manslaughter?" she asked.

"Anything up to 40 years. But if convicted she may end up in Rampton."

"Prison?"

"High security psychiatric hospital. Like Broadmoor, only for women. But yes, prison, in effect."

"There's one other thing that's puzzling me," said Andrew. "The tennis ball. Who did that?"

"Must have been someone who despised Lesley, I would think," said Manic.

"Imagine knowing she was dead and doing that!" Sara shuddered, along with Emerald. Then she screwed up her face in distaste and said, "But doesn't *rigor mortis* set in?"

"Not for a couple of hours," Feargal said quietly, looking at the delicate Emerald with concern.

Tamsin nodded. "It seems it has to be one of Toto, Amanda, or Glenda. Amanda and Toto were definitely there, and Glenda was due there too, but they didn't see her. Now, I know that Margaret and Glenda were having a set-to at the club last week. And I *think* that maybe Glenda had gone there, and passed Margaret's car leaving. She wouldn't even have seen the body in the ditch. She found no Amanda, who was late, and gave up and left again. So, putting two and two together, once the news got out, she questioned Margaret by the grass court, and decided to let her stew - not knowing whether she'd give the game away. She was glad to be rid of Lesley herself. No need to rock the boat. But that may have been a dangerous play. She could have been next on the list." She licked some icing off her finger. "Anyway, from what I overheard Amanda saying, it must have been Toto."

"But why?" said Sara.

"Apparently he was always nominating Glenda to be on the committee," Tamsin explained.

"And Lesley wouldn't hear of it," added Feargal.

"And Toto resented that." This from Emerald.

Sara looked puzzled. "Doesn't seem a strong motive ..."

"I imagine," explained Jonathan, "that he arrived at Tom's - don't know why - saw Lesley dead in the ditch, and took his opportunity to show his opinion of her."

"To get back at her?" asked Manic.

"Looks like it. He had no respect for the woman, alive or dead."

"Give me hedgehogs any day," sighed Manic.

"Or dogs!" said Tamsin.

"Or horses!" said Sara with a laugh.

"Or cats," ventured Emerald quietly.

"Or, indeed, cats," agreed Charity, whose three cats generously shared their home with her and Muffin.

"Actually, in my eyes Margaret's biggest crime was against cake!" said

Tamsin, lifting the big knife Kylie had put on the table. "Her cakes were dry and burnt and horrible."

"Nice to know where your priorities lie, Tamsin old bean!" chuckled Feargal.

"So let's tuck into this majestic cake from the Furies!" said Jonathan, licking his lips in anticipation, offering his plate for seconds.

"And let's hope we can actually enjoy some innocent tennis now!" said Tamsin. Jonathan, Sara, and Andrew all cried, "Here, here!" as Emerald reached for the plates and Tamsin plunged the knife through the tennis racquet on the cake, carefully avoiding the figure of her lovely dog.

Ready for the next book in the series? Check out https://mybook.to/ TamsinKernickCozies for all the latest books.

To find out how Tamsin arrived in Malvern and began Top Dogs, you can read this free novella "Where it all began" at

https://urlgeni.us/Lucyemblemcozy

and we'll be able to let you know when Tamsin's next adventure is ready for you!

And if you enjoyed this book, I'd love it if you could whiz over to where you bought it and leave a brief review, so others may find it and enjoy it as well, and be kind to their animals!

ALL THE TAMSIN KERNICK COZY ENGLISH MYSTERIES

Where it all began ..

https://urlgeni.us/Lucyemblemcozy

Sit, Stay, Murder! *

https://mybook.to/SitStayMurder

Ready, Aim, Woof! *

https://mybook.to/ReadyAimWoof

Down Dog! *

https://mybook.to/downdog

Barks, Bikes, and Bodies! *

https://mybook.to/BarksBikesBodies

Ma-ah, Ma-ah, Murder! *

https://mybook.to/TamsinKernickCozies

Snapped and Framed! *

https://mybook.to/SnappedFramed

Christmas Carols and Canine Capers! A Howling Good Christmas Mystery! *

https://mybook.to/Christmascozy

Game, Set, and Catch!

https://mybook.to/GameSetCatch

* Also available in Large Print

https://mybook.to/TamsinKernickCozies

ABOUT LUCY

From an early age I loved animals. From doing "showjumping" in the back garden with Simon, the long-suffering family pet - many years before Dog Agility was invented - I worked in the creative arts till I came back to my first love and qualified as a dog trainer.

Working for years with thousands of dogs and their colourful owners - from every walk of life - I found that their fancies and foibles, their doings and their undoings, served to inspire this series of cozy mysteries.

While the varying characters weave their way through the books, some becoming established personnel in the stories, the stars of the show are the animals!

They don't have human powers. They don't need to. They have plenty of powers of their own, which need only patience and kindness to bring out and enjoy with them.

If you enjoyed this story, I would LOVE it if you could hop over to where you purchased your book and leave a brief review!

Lucy Emblem

facebook.com/lucyemblemcozies

instagram.com/lucyemblem

bookbub.com/authors/lucy-emblem

Printed in Great Britain
by Amazon

57999766R00089